Seven Lean Years

Khalil Moh'd Khalil Hamad

Inner Child Press, ltd.

'building bridges of cultural understanding'

Credits

Author
Khalil Hamad

Introduction and Critical Analysis
Ibrahim Joher

Translators
Dr. Fayeq Oweis
Raneen Saadah

Editor
Fatima Abdel Kazim

Cover Design
Dr. Fayeq Oweis

General Information

Seven Lean Years

Khalil Moh'd Khalil Hamad

1st Edition: 2025

Publisher Information:
Inner Child Press International
www.innerchildpress.com

ISBN-13: 978-1-961498-71-6 (inner child press, ltd.)

$ 25.95

Table of Contents

Table of Contents . . . *continued*

Table of Contents . . . *continued*

Table of Contents ... *continued*

Table of Contents . . . *continued*

Table of Contents . . . *continued*

Epilogue
255

Seven Lean Years

Part Two of the Memoir of Khalil Hamad

This memoir offers a meticulous account of movement, dialogue, and suffering—so precise that it feels as though the writer is determined to etch every detail of his harrowing escape from Kuwait after the invasion of 1990 into memory.

Khalil Hamad, as revealed in these seven lean years, possesses a memory so vivid they evoke the legendary precision of Mohammad Hassanein Heikal, who could resurrect forgotten details from the depths of time.

The narrative voice here is intimate, almost conversational, though woven with Quranic phrases, colloquial proverbs, and echoes of prophetic tales. These barren years of Khalil's life are a trove of knowledge, offering readers both pleasure and insight. Khalil writes these pages in the ink of poverty, repeating the word—*poverty*—like a refrain, alongside the raw emotions and compromises that drive him to accept backbreaking labor, the meagerest wages, anything to break free from its grip.

Yet to brighten the mood for himself and for the reader who might be influenced as they empathize with the author's plight or recall their own struggles with hunger and helplessness, Khalil leavens his tale with dark humor (like describing the midnight trek to the outhouse with the whispered prayers and imagined monsters lurking in the dark), or perseverance to overcome poverty, or laboring without despair.

Through it all, Khalil's spirit remains restless—yearning for change, for a chance to serve society. He paves roads, builds schools, and extends kindness to his fellow breadwinners, those with modest education, when poverty forced him into the aluminum factory.

What strikes me most, however, was the pettiness and envy that plagued Khalil among his coworkers—whether at the village council or telecom office—led them to conspire against him, burdening him with tasks like cleaning the paint furnace. Through this, Khalil unveils a deeper societal illness: the corrosive jealousy and selfishness festering within the laboring class, stemming from ignorance and frustration. Such toxic behaviors call for urgent scrutiny; only by addressing their roots can we foster a fairer world built on empathy and mutual respect.

"Style is the man himself." This axiom perfectly encapsulates Khalil Hamad's prose. His writing mirrors his character and a singular intellect: a masterful interplay of humor and sorrow, enriched by vivid details and deliberate repetition, all woven with narrative tension. He hints at a crisis, then pauses—"This, I will unravel in its proper place"—drawing the reader ever deeper.

In short, this is a memoir rich in truth and meaning. Its message is clear: windows of joy open just when we've resigned ourselves to darkness.

My profound gratitude to Khalil Hamad—whose story moved me deeply, whose suffering I shared intimately, and whose experience, a vital thread in the tapestry of his people's struggle, I witnessed firsthand.

Esteemed Critic and Writer,

Ibrahim Joher

Seven Lean Years

Khalil Moh'd Khalil Hamad

Seven Lean Years

Refuge is Like Death

No one can fathom the bitterness of exile or grasp the pain it breeds until they have lived it—until they have been scorched by its fire and tasted its anguish. Only then does one truly understand the suffering, the torment, the devastation it leaves in its wake. This is the universal truth of all displacement, even its inverse: returning from exile to the embrace of homeland. But to be torn from your motherland and cast adrift in exile? That is when refuge becomes death.

My second son, Amjad, was born in Amman in mid-December 1990, while I remained stranded in Kuwait during my final, desperate preparations to escape that collapsing country. Upon reaching Jordan—after replacing the shattered windshield from that perilous return—I went first to see my wife and newborn. My family was still staying at the Hiyari villa in Al Rashid suburb, with my father-in-law's family. The sight of that infant, his luminous face and downy black hair, washed away some of the wounds of displacement and the torment of the grueling trip from Kuwait to Zarqa through the Traibeel border crossing.

Yet in those early days of return, I found myself consumed by another battle: shaking off the bone-deep chill that had seized me after my harrowing accident on my way back from Kuwait. Just beyond

Traibeel, my car's windshield had collapsed entirely, forcing me to drive the rest of the way unprotected from the desert's icy gales and howling eastern winds. To make matters worse, that ill-fated journey coincides with the early days of a brutal winter—a winter harsher than most, where snow fell in relentless waves and temperatures plunged to record lows.

I fought it with marathon sleep, hot infusions of sage, anise, and cinnamon—folk remedies steeped in the stubborn hope of warmth. Meanwhile, I had to wait for customs inspections in Zarqa to clear the shipment of belongings I had managed to salvage from Kuwait—a process that dragged on for two or three days, bogged down by the throngs of displaced families and their overstuffed trucks. Amid the chaos, a darkly comic farce unfolded: a customs officer insisted he could smell a fax machine hidden in our cargo, allegedly belonging to one of my shipping partners. The partner, of course, denied it—yet later whispered to us that if such a machine were found, he would gladly claim it.

Once the ordeal ended, I stored our salvaged belongings in a relative's garage in Bayader Wadi Al-Seer, biding time until we found a proper home. Then, I rejoined my family and my father in law's household, still crammed together in that Al Rashid suburb villa.

The physical toll of that torturous journey—and the horror of the accident—faded relatively quickly. But the psychic scars of fleeing Kuwait lingered, demanding patience, distraction, and time. At least my awareness of post-traumatic stress softened the blow somewhat.

I tried distracting myself by planting a winter garden in the villa's yard, but the project failed spectacularly—where not a single seedling thrived. Instead, I sought refuge in my car, escaping the villa's stifling crowds and the weight of exile. It became my movable sanctuary, a place to withdraw from the world.

I still remember one of those early days back in Jordan: craving a hearty meal, I bought half a grilled chicken from an eatery in Al Rashid suburb, then drove to a secluded spot overlooking the University of Jordan. There, alone in my car, I devoured that meal with ravenous delight—a small, almost ceremonial feast, made sacred by the deprivation we had endured since Kuwait's fall.

The car—which I was permitted to drive with my Iraqi-Kuwaiti black license plates—became my lifeline, allowing me to visit family and reconnect with relatives. During one of these early visits to meet a relative who owned a small grocery in Jabal Al Nuzha, I parked along the roadside just meters from his storefront. We sat together, this relative and I, getting acquainted since we had never met before. Only minutes had passed when we heard the shattering of glass. Moments later, it became clear that one of the children playing in the street—throwing stones at each other—had hurled a rock that reduced my rear windshield to splinters.

A group of boys—likely the stone-thrower's rivals—eagerly led me to his family's home. Given our dire financial situation and limited means at the time—and because I desperately needed the car during that bitterly cold winter, especially for transportation—I went with them to speak to the child's father.

The father greeted me with unexpected warmth and hospitality. I explained my financial strain frankly: If I had any money to replace the glass your son broke with his stone; I wouldn't have come knocking at your door. Ashamed to make such a request, I was relieved when he took responsibility without hesitation, urging me to repair the damage and bring him the bill. Not a flicker of resentment crossed his face.

The next day, I scoured the used auto parts markets in Marka, along Zarqa's highway, hunting for a Daihatsu windshield. When no used glass turned up—likely because the model was rare in Jordan—I had to buy a new one from a reputable shop for sixty dinars. My wife and I sold another piece of her gold jewelry to cover the cost until the boy's father could repay us.

Upon delivering the receipt the following day, the man received me graciously once more, reimbursing the full amount without hesitation or complaint. I thanked him for his decency and left, relieved to recover the money—a sum that meant everything to us at the time.

Naively, I thought that was the end of it—a tidy, happy resolution. But I would soon learn how wrong I was. There were depths to this situation I couldn't have imagined, and the man's kindness hid something else entirely. In time, I will share the rest of this strange tale—the shocking turn that threw me into an unthinkable crisis, the trap that nearly cost me dearly, and the friend who came to my rescue when I was still reeling from the aftermath of the Kuwait disaster. I will reveal the secret behind the ordeal, how it was resolved, and the unexpected hero who pulled me from the brink.

Thus began my lean years immediately after leaving Kuwait—a period marked by hardship, relentless challenges, and painful experiences aimed at severe financial strain and the withdrawal of relatives and friends. No sooner had I repaired the front windshield (believing its damage to be more chance) than the rear glass shattered again—this time deliberately. This second breakage might have cost me dearly and had it not been for God's mercy and the wisdom of a friend who understood such matters and rushed to my aid.

O Father! Do as you are commanded.
You will find me, if Allah wills,
of the steadfast.
(Surah As-Saffat 37:102)

I am now convinced that my seven lean years began because I defied the old saying, "Bite the bullet"—and worse, my disobedience to my father's guidance in a moment I foolishly believed his counsel could be bypassed without consequence. At the time, it seemed trivial, a minor divergence that couldn't possibly alter the trajectory of my life or tip the scales between success and ruin.

Now I know better. The universe shifts when a son disregards his father's will, when he ignores his guidance and follows his own desires—even if disobedience comes cloaked in necessity. His life, no matter how pure his intentions, no matter how desperate his excuses, becomes a living torment.
But the opposite is also true. When a son submits—when he yields to his father's wish, stifling his own longing, even if obedience feels like stepping into fire—the world bends to aid him.

Then the universe realigns itself to open the gates of heaven for the son, fulfilling his desires. At times, miracles may unfold in his favor—bending the rhythm of his life to obedience, answering his deepest longings, and granting his most fervent wishes. Divine intervention may even ransom the son, as it did in an ancient time when he bowed his neck to his father's blade and said, "O father, do as you are commanded. You will find me, if Allah wills, of the steadfast." (Surah As-Saffat 37:102). For redemption comes only through absolute surrender to the father's will.

I was the youngest son of Zainab's children, and as the last-born, I was cradled in the tender love and care of my parents—the privilege of the final bud on the branch. This was the love my father gave me all my life, especially after my mother's untimely passing. I loved him devoutly, obeyed him without question. Never once, in any matter of consequence, did I defy his will—save for that single act of disobedience. And though I could not have known it then, that one rebellion would later draw down upon me a tide of misfortunes, casting me into the long, barren tunnel of lean years. Yet the true cause—the unseen blow that first condemned me to that darkness—had already fallen years before my defiance, a punishment awaiting its hour.

None of this would have happened if I had just denied myself—my desires—and yielded to his request, obedient and compliant, even if it meant embarrassment or defying social norms.

Let me recount the moment of my rebellion:

It began with family and kin gathered at my bidding, all preparing to visit the home of my father in law, to seek his daughter's hand and recite Al-Fatiha. But fate wove another thread into that hour: my uncle, Yusuf Al-Asaad, had just returned from a journey to Palestine, where he had met my father. A message had been entrusted to him—one he carried back to Kuwait, arriving that very noon. He joined the gathering as the procession readied itself, but as we prepared to depart for the would-be bride's home, he drew close and whispered:

'Your father charged me to tell you—he forbids you to marry a girl without residency in Palestine.' And with that, the matter was sealed.

A shudder ran through me. I stiffened where I stood, turning as if caught in a whirlwind, lost for a moment in the storm of my thoughts. A deep, gnawing doubt took hold—but then I steadied myself. 'Too late,' I told him. 'Had it reached me before the Al-Fatiha was agreed upon, I might have heeded it. But to turn back now, after pledging my word before all these witnesses, would shame me before all.'

And so it came to pass. We moved forward with the marriage arrangements, and in time, the wedding was celebrated with joy, laughter, and merriment. Yet, no matter how brightly the days shone, I could never outrun the shadow of my deepest fears—fears born of defying my father's will in that fateful moment. They clung to me like my own silhouette, whispering that sorrow and ruin would surely follow.

And follow they did. Before three years of marriage had passed—a union I suspect never pleased my father, for it had spurned his wise and far-seeing counsel—Kuwait was suddenly thrown into chaos. Without warning, without omens, the world erupted. The cataclysm that followed forced me to flee that stricken land, to escape the devastation and save myself, leaving all behind to seek refuge with my family in Jordan.

That day, I resolved to leave at once for Jordan, though I knew I would likely face problems with residency and work. At the time, I held only the Green Card—issued to me as a temporary procedural formality upon my return from studies in the United States, with the promise that it would later be replaced by the main border administration upon review.

The Jordanian Ministry of Interior had granted me the Green Card (for Palestinians abroad) despite my presenting documents proving I had worked in Kuwait since mid-1978 before traveling to America. My entry into the West Bank was solely to renew my time-limited permit before returning to my job in Kuwait—a circumstance that, under Jordanian regulatory procedures, should have qualified me for the Yellow Card (for Palestinians working abroad temporarily), which grants residency and work rights in Jordan.

After my forced return, I exhausted every effort to exchange the Green Card for the Yellow Card as Jordanian officials had promised. I submitted evidence, following proper procedures, that I had been abroad for work before the separation order. But the political turmoil following the Kuwait crisis left no room for appeals.

The green card became a Jordanian-imposed barricade, shutting every door of opportunity for seven long, grueling years. My family and I suffered immensely during that time, tasting the bitter sting of poverty, the harshness of life, and its unrelenting grind. Those years deserved—without exaggeration—to be called 'the lean years,' and one of the chief reasons for our suffering was my failure to secure a decent, fitting job that could provide a reasonable income.

And of course, those seven years were rich with events—with bitter, dramatic trials, hardships, and cruel twists of fate. The scarcity of money and the steady decline of our circumstances carved a deep and lasting place in memory. In time, I will recount them all to you, one after another, in their full detail: stirring, sorrowful, and shocking in almost every way.

Then, suddenly, fortune turned when those seven lean years finally passed. On that day, I succeeded in reclaiming the yellow card through official channels, submitting the necessary documents to the concerned authorities in a routine, effortless procedure that required no extraordinary measures. And as if fate had conspired in my favor, this coincided with another joyous event that lifted me from the crucible of need and despair.

It is worth nothing that I lived through those seven long years without a valid passport—refusing to relinquish my right to citizenship, and thus, under the prevailing laws, forfeiting any claim to permanent residency. My struggle to reclaim the yellow identity card years later is a tale so astonishing, and unbelievable, that I will recount in full later as the story unfolds. That moment restored my soul, flung open the doors of opportunity, and marked the beginning of the end for those bitter years of hardship.

But first, let me take you back—chronologically— through the gripping, harrowing details of those seven lean years, where my family and I tasted the bitterness of deprivation and endured suffering beyond measure.

Let me take you back to the start!

Mere days after arriving in Jordan, once the brief respite of rest had passed, I began my search for work—despite my fears that securing any official employment would be impossible due to the obstacle of the Green Card. Still, I spared no effort, leaving no door unknocked, no opportunity untried. I had hoped that my wife's Jordanian citizenship—coupled with her lack of residency in the West Bank—might help circumvent the Green Card obstacle amid the refugee crisis. But even that proved futile. No mercy was shown, no reprieve from the humiliation of begging for work to spare me the humiliation of destitution.

Meanwhile, the doors to Kuwait had sealed shut entirely, severing all hope of return. With resources dwindling and prospects fading, my father-in-law surrendered the furnished villa—his own funds exhausted—and we moved into a small basement apartment in Bayader Wadi Al-Seer for a hundred dinars a month. My uncle's family, my father-in-law, relocated to a modest flat provided by a relative, from the Al-Khatib family, in the same area.

By then, we were selling the last of my wife's gold jewelry to cover our most urgent needs—especially those of the children. No money came to us from any source, not even as charity.

Day by day, our situation worsened. The world, vast as it was, seemed to close in around us. I did not know how to escape the tragic predicament I found myself in—my wife and children unable to enter Palestine (not that it was a desirable option to begin with), and I, unable to secure even the most basic income to sustain us. More than once, I considered leaving my family behind to seek work elsewhere, if only to put bread on the table.

At times, I blamed myself for leaving Kuwait, despite the mortal dangers of staying. Other times, I resented my wife for demanding my return under threatening to join me in that wretched land.

Until we hit rock bottom. My wife's gold was nearly gone when a relative informed me that the company he worked for needed an employee—someone to work on a telex machine. It was a position beneath even a secretary's rank, with meager pay and no qualifications required beyond typing.

I seized the opportunity at once. At the interview, I concealed my credentials. When asked about my degrees, I claimed I had barely completed high school 'Tawjihi'—lest my higher qualifications disqualify me from the pitifully paid job.

I began right after passing the typing test, but within days, I nearly lost the position. Why? What happened after I secured the job? How did the manager realize I was overqualified? What was his reaction, and how did he respond when my credentials caught his attention?

Telex Operator Job

Finding work had become my sole obsession as the days dragged on. When I heard of an opening—a telex operator position—at that prestigious international trading company headquartered in the Housing Bank Complex, I rushed to apply. The job was humble, even menial by professional standards, with meager pay. But to me, after months of harsh deprivation following the Kuwait invasion and my sudden unemployment, it was a glimmer of hope. I accepted it without hesitation, despite its glaring mismatch with my advanced academic qualifications and years of experience—and despite the meager income it offered.

The hours I spent facing the wall in that cramped storage room behind the telex machine - where the telegraph operator sat - didn't faze me. I had worked as a porter during my university years in the United States, and I had enough self-assurance and resilience to swallow my pride and endure this wretched situation I found myself in. I could accept it, even live with it, under the weight of circumstance and the pressing need for income.

A relative who worked at the company arranged an interview with the operations manager. We agreed not to disclose my advanced degrees, lest I be deemed overqualified. At the interview, when asked about my education, I claimed I had barely finished high school but could type quickly out of habit and experience.

The manager put me to the test that day—a trial by fire, or rather, by telex. He assigned me to type several texts in the form of telex messages. Thanks to my advanced typing course and my experience with computers dating back to my student days in America. Later, as a translator, I'd spent countless hours transcribing texts, my fingers flying across the keys until speed and precision became second nature.

The supervising manager who examined my work noticed precisely this - he was impressed by my performance, my speed, and the few typographical errors I made. Without hesitation, he offered me the position, suggesting I start at the earliest opportunity. He informed me the salary would be 150 Jordanian dinars—the absolute minimum, barely more than what janitors earned.

Of course, this job and its accompanying salary represented a tremendous breakthrough—a lifeline for a broken man emerging from Kuwait's devastation empty-handed, surviving only on his wife's dwindling gold reserves. After suffering immensely just to put bread on the table for my family, I accepted the offer immediately. I didn't negotiate the salary or make any additional demands. To me, this offer was like oxygen to someone on life support. At the very least, that meager sum would cover the rent and some of our most urgent necessities—baby formula, diapers—while helping to stop, even partially, the financial bleeding before the last of our gold vanishes.

The next day, I threw myself into the work with voracious dedication. As expected, my duties were limited to typing paychecks for the company's thirty-plus employees. These men worked tirelessly corresponding with foreign firms—requesting quotes, inquiring about prices, negotiating terms, and tracking shipments—all the myriad tasks essential to our business. The company served as a middleman, supplying everything from sewing needles to complete machines, from everyday garments to traditional djellaba, bringing these goods to both local and Gulf markets for agreed-upon commissions.

I resigned myself to that cramped, isolated storage room, working in silent obscurity, nearly invisible. I kept my head down and avoided drawing attention—terrified my qualifications and past experience might be discovered, knowing such exposure could cost me my job.

I leveraged my expertise in English, my swift typing skills, my knowledge of import-export operations and commercial correspondence—gained from my work in the Letters of Credit department at Burgan Bank—to refine the company's correspondence with foreign entities. I had even authored a training manual on crafting polished English business letters, distinguished by its elegant style. A university professor, a friend of mine, later adopted it as a teaching resource for his business correspondence course.

I quickly proved my worth to the company, especially since many employees struggled with English, their correspondence riddled with broken, clumsy language that failed to convey even basic clarity. One employee even wrote "S" before "I" in the word "Is." I was later stunned to learn that the lowest salary paid to sales representatives—whose letters I typed—was no less than seven hundred Jordanian dinars, with some surpassing a thousand. There were reasons existed, of course.

Only a few days into my new position, diligently refining the language of correspondence and polishing the communication skills, when a reply arrived from a German company in response to an inquiry I had sent regarding pricing for certain products related to one of the company's departments. Their letter contained words that made my pulse quicken: "We recognize that your company is substantial by virtuc of the exceptional English used in the correspondence we have received from you."

A copy of this incoming message had reached the company's director—Mr. Sharawy, of course. As was customary, he reviewed all incoming and outgoing correspondence. So it was no surprise when he stormed into the telex room, clutching the letter in one hand while pressing the other to his mouth in a gesture of sheer astonishment. His face twisted with agitation as he fixed me with a sharp, interrogative tone:

"What in God's name did you study? What degrees do you even have?"

Holding to the adage "Honesty is salvation," I hesitated, then confessed:

"I hold a master's in English Literature from the University of San Diego, California—in the United States. In Kuwait, I served as translation officer for Yusuf Ahmed Al-Ghanim company, and before that, I worked in a bank's documentary credits department." I summarized my experience tersely.
"And my bold display of my qualifications was not only because of that letter of praise I had received. I feared my credentials might have reached him somehow. After all, who knows? As the saying goes: "If a secret goes beyond two, it spreads."

So shocked was he that he could only clutch his head in disbelief. He spun halfway around, then jerked back to where he had stood, pacing rapidly back and forth before finally fixing me with a stare. His face darkened, twisting into a scowl. For a moment he seemed caught in some private dilemma, weighing his thoughts as he spoke:

"Sir, this means you should be sitting in my chair! Not working as a telex operator!"

With that, he stormed out of the room, leaving behind the unmistakable impression—through his theatrically explosive reaction—that my time with the company might very well be over.

That day, I returned home ridden by demons of grief and worry. Sorrow clawed at my rest, puzzling up and down, bracing for the manager's decision now that the truth about my qualifications had been laid bare. The question haunted me:

Would this man overlook the fact that I was overqualified for the position and let me keep working? Or would he terminate my employment—barely begun at his company after only a handful of days?

I braced myself for dismissal. As the proverb goes, my cheek has grown accustomed to the blows. Already I was calculating how to provide for my family if let go, dreading a return to the harsh unemployment that followed Kuwait's invasion. What was the manager's decision? I wonder.

Ordeals Are Gifts:
The Most Tested Reap the Greatest Glory

O people, who endure hardships and trials—do not despair. Know that these pains and sorrows were meant to strengthen you, to forge resilience within your soul. The most tested among men are the prophets, then the righteous, then those of virtue. No calamity befalls a person, no darkness swallows them like the depths of a well, no prison confines them, except that a greater good is decreed for them—good in this world and the next. Gold is refined by fire, a man is tested by adversity, and a diamond is forged under pressure and heat.

And here I am, like Prophet Joseph—this is my story, my path of suffering. I endured the cruelest trials of childhood, its sorrows and pains. I was struck by the sting of early orphanhood, tasted the bitterness of loss, and through it all, my grief and anguish forged me into someone strong, proud, and self-made—a man of resolve and wisdom.

Then came the bitterness of exile, a well of estrangement I drank from for over ten relentless years. And yet, this ordeal granted me clarity, depth, and bestowed upon me countless traits and abilities. My Lord, in His mercy, spared me the confines of a prison—had I known its solitude, perhaps I, too, would have interpreted dreams like Prophet Joseph. Still, through all this suffering, I emerged with an insight known only to those who have tasted loss and afflictions.

True, I did not gain the power to interpret visions, nor did I become a trustee over the treasures of the land. But in all honesty, I have always felt cradled in God's protection, certain that my trials were but preparation for something greater.

And so it proved. I formulated a pioneering theory, introducing an unprecedented perspective and unveiling the hidden wellspring of creative energy. My Positronic Theory posits a direct correlation between pain and creativity—that orphanhood, as the greatest source of suffering, and creativity share a cause-and-effect relationship.

This was the theory that affirmed Gibran Khalil Gibran's assertion that 'a pearl is a temple built by pain around a grain of sand.' I demonstrated the validity and credibility of this theory through research evidence and statistical data that astonishingly confirmed my hypotheses, proving the relationship extends far beyond mere coincidence.

Moreover, I had developed a certain sensitivity—a transparency of perception, a sharp intuition—that allowed me, at times, to glimpse the future, to read the secrets of souls, and to decipher the unspoken words in people's eyes. Perhaps, at appropriate moments throughout these memoirs, I'll share few of these funny moments that life threw my way. And let me be clear: this is no heresy, no divination, no sophistry. Rather, as my theory suggests, these are a mental acuity born of pain and tribulation.

Admittedly, I tried wielding this foresight—along with my knowledge of body language and human personality traits—to gauge the manager's stance when I revealed my qualifications, which by most standards were overqualified for a role as mundane as operating a telex machine. Yet I couldn't quite decipher his true reaction. Would he let me keep the job? Or dismiss me outright? His initial response gave no clear signal. Still, I sensed he was concealing something—an intent I couldn't yet name. Though his features held a glimmer of cryptic amusement, they hinted at words left unspoken.

Because " a burnt child dreads the fire," and reeling from the shock that had struck me and my family after Kuwait's catastrophe—terrified of returning to the square of unemployment and severed income— I sank into despair after that revelation. Anxiety took hold of me as a cloud of grief enveloped me that day, growing heavier when night drew its curtains. I lay awake thinking of what might become of me. The next day I went to work, wary of the possibility my job might end. But I steadied myself, walked to the telex machine, and continued typing messages as usual—as if yesterday's storm had never broken.

An hour passed, then two, then three—yet everything remained normal. No one came to question me; no one even glanced my way. Still, anxiety gnawed at me as I braced for the unknown. And though the silence brought no tragic news, with each passing moment, a quiet reassurance settled deeper into my heart.

And at midday, as I sat in my cubicle behind the telex machine, I heard the booming voice of a man—unfamiliar, thunderous, out of place in these surroundings—drawing nearer, heading straight for the office of the company's general manager, just steps from where I sat. It soon became clear that he was a towering figure, broad-shouldered and powerfully built, exuding the air of a military general. His presence commanded the room, undeniable, even behind thick, heavy glasses.

Before long, whispers began spreading like wildfire through the company's corridors. Speculations swirled about the reason behind that thunderous presence. It was then that I learned the man was the brother-in-law of the company's director—one of the Al-Natsha family. He had come because the director decided to establish a new department for trading used auto parts, placing this man at its helm. More often than not, that decision was nothing but the company director's attempt to help his brother-in-law—who, as it later transpired, had also fallen victim to Kuwait's economic collapse. Upon his return, he suffered devastating losses after investing his entire capital in establishing a state-of-the-art apiary in the Jerash region. But before long, the varroa mite—that deadly scourge of honeybees—wiped out the entire apiary. This catastrophe left our man bankrupt, joining the ranks of jobless victims of misfortune.

It was evident from the man's bearing that he possessed exceptional managerial and leadership experience—the unmistakable air of a seasoned executive. Yet it soon became clear that his Achilles' heel was his lack of English proficiency. Seizing on this, the General Manager issued an administrative decree that very moment, coinciding with the establishment of the new department. The order reassigned me as assistant to Mr. Al-Natsha, General Manager of Automotive Spare Parts, with my responsibilities to include—among other duties—overseeing foreign correspondence and providing necessary administrative support.

In a single moment, that decision changed me from a mere telex operator—isolated in my cramped storage-room cloister, face to the wall—into the assistant general manager of a startup, dealing in auto parts, under the parent company's umbrella.

Only then did I understand what the general manager had concealed when I revealed my qualifications. That shrewd man had seized the opportunity my education and experience presented, using them to complete the construction of the auto parts division. He must have been contemplating this for some time, and my arrival solved his dilemma—his deputy's weak English skills had left a gap I was now filling.

Overnight, I became the assistant to the general manager of the auto parts division under the General Products Trading Company. I did not disappoint their hopes or trust. In record time, I corresponded with multiple suppliers, compiled a database of quotes and specifications on the computer, and identified the best sources and prices. Soon, Mr. Al-Natsha began ordering container after container of used parts and engines, transforming the company into one of the largest local players in the market. At times, entire shipments were sold at sea—proof of the reputation and efficiency we had built.

Yet, despite my pivotal role in establishing a new production line for the parent company—a venture I doubt would have materialized without my contributions—and despite eventually receiving a raise of hundred Jordanian dinars, my salary upon leaving after four years was a meager 250 dinars. As the saying goes, "Bite the bullet"—but that income remained below the poverty line, barely covering basic needs. Those years drained what little savings and gold my wife had left. As for my departure from the company, it was the pinnacle of misery and pain. The events I will recount, God willing, are enough to make the blood run cold.

To his credit, Mr. Al-Natsha always treated me with respect, valued my qualifications and experience, and trusted my capabilities. Not once in those four years did he belittle or wrong me. But what etched his memory indelibly in my mind was not his professionalism—it was an act of kindness, like saving a drowning man. And in that moment, I was the drowning man, and he, the rescuer.

Time's Trials Never Cease

My return to Jordan as an immigrant from Kuwait began with brutal hardship. On my very first day back, my car was vandalized—both front and rear windows shattered. Yet, despite its condition, that car became my lifeline, ferrying me across Amman's sprawling neighborhoods. I drove to the remote Al Hashemiya district, where my cousin Taysir Salem Abu Hammad lived. Then crisscrossed the city's heart: The University of Jordan area, Al Jubeiha, Abu Nseir, Wadi Shueib, Abu Al Sous, Marj Al Hamam, Wadi Al-Seer, and the airport road. These places became my anchors. Though we lived in strained circumstances and money was scarce, we still ventured out for picnics where we would eat, laugh, and sometimes forage for wild herbs in Al Jubeiha's fields, where we gathered mustard greens. The children's amusement park there became our regular haunt.

Landing a job during those dire days felt like a miracle. It salvaged my family from the brink of destitution—a hairsbreadth from begging—and for a fleeting moment, life smiled. That job was our sole lifeline in those early post-return days.

Yet life's cruelties are relentless. Just as hope flickers, the blow comes harder. Weeks barely passed in my new position at the General Products Trading Company when the news arrived: my father—may he rest in peace—had passed. Bedridden since 1987 after a stroke left him fully paralyzed and speechless, I'd last seen him in 1989 when my cousin Mohammad Salem Abu Hammad warned of his deteriorating state. I stayed by his side for a month of unending torment—not just from witnessing his suffering, but from the military patrols storming our home night and day. The stories from that month, with their harrowing details of hardship, terror, and brushes with death, could fill an action thriller. I'll recount them in their chilling entirety when the time comes, God willing, as the narrative unfolds.

He was my father, my compass, half the love I'd ever known. Yet I didn't attend his burial. Even now, I can't say why—perhaps the new job's demands, my empty pockets, or the rushed funeral held to honor his soul, which had slipped away at dusk. Had I left the next morning, I'd have been too late.

It came as no surprise that this seismic loss struck at life's most vulnerable hour. Misfortune never comes alone—it strikes in relentless waves, as experience teaches and history solemnly attests. Imam Al-Shafi'i's timeless words echoed through my grief:

'The trials of time are endless, unceasing,
Yet its joys arrive like fleeting holidays.'

As if the wounds of our forced exile from Kuwait weren't enough, the calamity of my father's death came to pile misery upon misery—deepening our grief, our pain, our despair, our destitution, and all the scars left behind by the disaster of Kuwait. It brought fresh sorrow, fresh agony, a gnawing guilt, the searing sting of loss, the death of my last pillar of support, and the withering of half the love that had remained in my life after my mother's early departure. Thus, my orphanhood was absolute. They say losing both parents is to lose the hands that held you.

The year 1991 passed with its sweetness and bitterness, its blessings and curses—though the bitterness far outweighed the sweetness, and the curses overshadowed the blessings. Were it not for the children, and later finding work, its darkness would have been absolute.

As days passed, working with Mr. Natsha gradually became a surprisingly enjoyable routine, for it carried in its nature both challenge and opportunity for creativity and diligence.

As for the winter of 1992, it proved exceptionally harsh by Jordanian standards that season. Snow fell abundantly, recurring seven separate times, accumulating to window-height in Bayader Wadi Al-Seer—nearly a full meter deep.

The worsening cold amplified our hardships, stretching our meager budget further as we scrambled to afford heating. Like squirrels preparing for winter, we would stock up on fuel, bread, and essentials whenever weather warnings predicted snowfall.

During one of these snowstorms, the kerosene in our heater ran out suddenly—far too early—and we hadn't stored any extra. With children in the house who needed warmth, I had no choice but to go fetch more on foot, now that all car traffic had stopped.

The truth is, walking on snow-packed streets becomes nearly impossible, especially in the early morning hours. That winter, the icy conditions around the Osh Al Hana restaurant turned the sidewalk into a dark comedy—people toppling over like dominoes in a scene both hilarious and pathetic. The compacted snow had turned into treacherous sheets of black ice, precisely the kind the meteorological department had warned about. Mornings rendered these paths virtually impassable. The cruel humor lay in how each fallen soul would scramble upright, terrified of being seen in such undignified humiliation, only to immediately lose footing again.

That afternoon, I decided to walk to Al Dajani Gas Station near the Seventh Circle to fetch kerosene. But when I arrived, I found the nearest station had run dry. So I turned toward Mecca Street, heading to the Sindbad station instead. There, I finally filled my yellow plastic jerrycan and began the journey back home to the Bayader—on foot, just as I'd come. At times, I carried the jerrycan on my shoulder; at others, I dragged it with effort. Then I noticed the ornamental palm trees lining the street's median. I broke off a piece of their fronds and fashioned a rope to tie around the jerrycan's handle, pulling it over the snow. But the coarse palm leaves gouged a deep cut into my hand. I pressed a fistful of pristine white snow to the wound, watching as it stained crimson, the blood vivid against the ice. I went—walking, resting, dragging the jerrycan, then hoisting it back onto my shoulder—until I reached the Seventh Circle on my return. There, by chance, a small pickup truck passed by. The driver, kindhearted, loaded all those heading to the Bayader into the back, myself included, my yellow jerrycan in tow. And so, that respectful stranger ended my ordeal, delivering me—and the kerosene—home on that bitterly cold, snow-laden day.

We emerged from that winter unscathed, and the world seemed on the verge of smiling at us—despite the still-fresh wounds of shock and loss simmering in our chests. Work was progressing smoothly, without a hitch; everything was perfectly in place. We even had enough money to get by, with some to spare. Yet we hadn't fully escaped the grip of pain—such is the way of this world, its unrelenting nature. And so, it was only a matter of time before trials found us again. That day, the phone rang. On the other end, a voice belonging to someone close to me delivered words that struck me with brutal force, leaving me stunned, adrift in confusion. How would I find my way out of this? Salvation, it turned out, would come at the hands of Mr. Al-Natsha.

March to the Beat of One's Own Drum

My work at the General Products Trading Company marked my first true foray into the mercantile world. There, under the mentorship of Mr. Al-Sha'rawi, I learned the closely guarded secrets of trade and wealth accumulation. He was that rare breed of man—a visionary, a genius, a risk-taker, blessed with extraordinary managerial abilities, leadership qualities, and a commercial mind that bordered on brilliance.

What struck me most about this man—who, I later learned, had become a millionaire at a remarkably young age—was his exceptional ability to listen. He encouraged others to share their ideas openly, welcoming even the most outlandish proposals with initial enthusiasm. Then he'd disappear—perhaps for a day, two, or three—but the idea would linger in his mind like a stew simmering on low heat. He'd turn it over carefully, examining every angle, letting it mature slowly. If it proved worthwhile, he'd seize it with both hands. But if he sensed it lacked merit, he'd return with a reasoned explanation—clear, logical, and devoid of condescension— never leaving the idea's proposer feeling slighted or discouraged.

As for the qualities that I believe led him to become one of those millionaires: his courage, his love of adventure, his unconventional and risk-taking mindset, his decisiveness, and his patience—it was as if anger simply couldn't find its way to him.

He once told me personally that he might have been the first foreigner to visit China in 1965—that ancient empire which welcomed him with unparalleled hospitality, rolling out the red carpet and treating him throughout his travels during China's early days of openness with the same refined courtesy reserved for heads of state.

He told me that when he first visited China for trade purposes, the country lacked any bank capable of handling documentary transactions for export and import operations. He had urged Chinese officials to establish their first commercial bank for this specific purpose. By necessity, he became their advisor in this field, assisting them in founding China's first commercial bank there—an institution that would implement documentary credits following the standard practices of international banks.

He explained to me that he had been among the first businessmen to strike commercial deals with China. With shrewd vision, he proposed manufacturing the "Gulf Thobe" to his own exact specifications. This made him a primary supplier of the traditional garment to Gulf markets from the 1960s through the 1990s. His ventures didn't stop there: he stood among the earliest foreigners to establish his own factory in China, producing goods at minimal cost.

As time passed, his business ventures with China expanded significantly. He began manufacturing various types of garments and fabrics there, establishing brand names that soon dominated the growing markets. Before long, he had become a millionaire at a remarkably young age. His pharmacy degree was set aside, forgotten like an old prescription, as he abandoned his early career in Kuwait's pharmaceutical field during his youth.

I later learned he had established a factory in China that produced goods for a very specific clientele. The factory would operate for a set period each year, then shutter its doors completely. This cycle repeated indefinitely - all to ensure these exclusive products never fell into the hands of anyone outside the intended buyers. These privileged customers, through prior arrangement with him, would purchase the entire output.

Though he began his career in textiles, specializing in djellaba, he later expanded into diverse commercial ventures. He became a commission agent supplying every imaginable commodity - from sewing needles to computers, from sewing machines—including German-made Union Special machines, with which I shared an interesting story I will recount in due time—to automotive parts, a sector I personally helped him establish. Yet his core business remained commission-based clothing trade for local and Gulf markets.

This extraordinary man had amassed a staggering fortune through a devilishly clever scheme and sharp business acumen. He would, for instance, purchase fabric at seven dollars per meter, only to sell it at fourteen dollars per meter—but he didn't stop at mere repetition. Instead, he took a swatch of the same cloth and scoured factory warehouses for rejected stock—bolts of fabric deemed defective by automated systems for the slightest variation in color shade. Computers would flag these as non-compliant, consigning them to storage to be sold as scrap or destroyed. Seizing the opportunity, he bought up such "flawed" inventory at a fraction of the cost and resold it at market price. No one ever noticed the minute discrepancy in hue, and thus, he reaped colossal profits.

Inspired by this atmosphere, and with my growing expertise in commerce, I found myself chasing my dream of wealth. I began contemplating the establishment of a factory to produce men's undergarments under global brand names—a venture that was quite popular at the time. After all, it required no more than eight German "Union Special" sewing machines, which the company already imported. Jordan, back then, was experiencing a boom in that very industry. Seeking counsel, I approached Mr. Al-Sha'rawi, the company's director, and asked his opinion of the idea. He offered me a pointed piece of advice: not to wade into production. To him, it would be like swimming in the open sea—where a man could easily slip beneath the waves, drowning in the exhausting demands of the enterprise. Skilled labor, he stressed, would be indispensable, and that in itself was a tremendous responsibility, a problem nearly impossible to control. If I insisted on venturing into business, he advised, I should stick to buying and selling, steering clear of production in all its forms.

No doubt, his experience and knowledge lent weight to his warnings about the risks of working in production—a lesson tragically illustrated by his brother-in-law, Al-Natsha. The man had established an apiary for honey production, only to be ruined in a night with no dawn by a tiny, barely known pest no larger than a pinhead: the varroa mite. The devastation was catastrophic.

As for Mr. Al-Natsha, despite his leadership qualities, strong personality, and financial expertise as a professional accountant, after that staggering loss he resorted to working as an employee for his brother-in-law. I couldn't help but think that Shakespeare's saying: "A jack of all trades and master of none" applied perfectly to him.

Yet though he never attained the wealth his brother-in-law amassed, the man radiated wisdom—and where wisdom thrives, goodness follows. He was a living treasury of proverbs, armed with the perfect adage for every occasion. Among his most frequent refrains was: "March to the beat of one's own drum," and another saying he'd often repeat: "Wishes won't wash dishes."

He undoubtedly possessed deep knowledge of tribal customs and clan leadership—I myself had benefited from his shrewdness, wisdom, and knowledge in such matters. It was when my relative, the shop owner in Jabal Al-Nuzha, called me. I had been visiting him at the time, my car parked outside his store, when its rear window was shattered. Back then, the child's father had willingly, even cheerfully, paid for the damage without the slightest hesitation or resentment. That had been over a year before this unexpected call.

My relative explained: according to the man's customary law, I ought to have returned the money he had paid. The demand stunned me. Never had I encountered such a tradition—had I known repayment was expected, let alone that it would later cost me exponentially through ceremonial compensation and tribal dues, I would have left the car window broken through freezing winds or sold the vehicle outright.

I felt truly trapped. I had no money whatsoever to cover the costs of these absurd rituals—practices God Himself never ordained. In desperation, I rushed to seek help from Mr. Al-Natsha, a Southerner who still navigated these tribal customs effortlessly, unlike us Northerners. He asked for the man's phone number and called him as I listened intently. After the customary greetings, the real conversation began. Mr. Al-Natsha firmly told him he had no right to hold me accountable based on his own traditions and tribal codes, that he should have respected my customs, and understood my ignorance of such matters. Then the threat, delivered like honey on a blade: "But if you insist, three hundred Hebron elders and I will visit you. Though we'll return your sixty dinars with warmth."

The man relented. Just like that, Mr. Al-Natsha pulled me from the jaws of a crisis that could've cost me dearly in an already precarious time—had that man enforced his tribal law. Later, I repaid the sixty dinars as agreed, and the matter ended there. But the sting of it never left me. A sense of injustice still smolders in my chest. After that incident, I grew wary of stumbling into similar traps, even considering fleeing regions governed by custom rather than law. If tribal justice forced me to repay money for a window someone else broke, I shuddered, what would it demand for something graver—God forbid—like an accident?

The day after that unforgettable ordeal, the company decided to discard old samples and offered them to employees. Among my share were a few children's garments. But the young office messenger—nephew of the company owner, a boy whose father I'd once met, a dervish-like man who fasted like the Prophet David—found a sleek black knee-length jacket in the pile. Jokingly, I offered to buy it from him for two dinars. He agreed without hesitation. That jacket became my armor against winter's bite for over a decade. Was it his need for those two dinars that made him agree? Or did he, a simple errand boy, yield it out of kindness to me, the salaried employee? I still remember another day when that same young man was feeding paper into the shredder. Suddenly, the machine snatched the necktie he was wearing that day, nearly strangling him. Had he not reacted quickly and stopped the machine, it might have ended badly. When he pulled the tie free, its end had been shredded into frayed strands, like the tail of a horse.

Not long after, I was forced to relinquish my car— a loss that rendered life widow-like, a private hell.

And then, a small mouse suddenly appeared in our home. I killed it brutally, but my wife saw its arrival as an omen of departure. She insisted on this—that the mouse's appearance was no coincidence, that behind it lay something momentous, without a doubt. And indeed, it happened just as she said, astonishing me completely not long after.

There's a Mouse on the Loose in Our House!

I can assure you, dear readers, that our apartment's walls had no crevice wide enough for even the smallest cockroach to slip through. The windows were secured with mesh screens, and the drains—sealed tightly with iron covers—were entirely internal. Yet, to our astonishment, we awoke one morning to find an audacious little mouse scurrying about our home as though it had declared the place its sovereign territory.

We searched frantically, turning the place upside down, but found no breach through which the wretched intruder could have entered. How it infiltrated our sanctuary remained a mystery. After a fierce chase, I finally cornered the creature in a tight space and delivered its demise—brutally—with the sole of my shoe.

That incident might have passed like a fleeting shadow, nothing more than a trivial occurrence—after all, the apartment was on the ground floor, and only the Almighty never errs. Perhaps that wretched mouse had slipped in through the main door in a moment of inattention. But the real problem that emerged from this encounter was my wife's reaction. The instant she saw the mouse, her face flushed with a mixture of anger, sorrow, and agitation, and she blurted out with raw spontaneity:

"Oh God, this is a sign—we will have to leave this apartment!" She spoke as though she were stating an irrefutable truth, as if she had lived through this exact omen before.

But under the weight of shock, my precarious finances, the fragile stability —lacking both the means and necessary funds for relocation, with apartment rents being exorbitant and relocation inevitably costly—I rushed to dismiss it as mere superstition. 'This is an omen we cannot heed,' I insisted. "A rat cannot possibly be some divine emissary delivering eviction notices. Never in our family's history has such nonsense been heard—this is pure fabrication!" My words were a desperate attempt to slam shut any discussion of departure, to uproot the very idea of leaving from its foundations. My original intention had been to banish the idea from my wife's mind entirely. Yet instead, it took root in mine. In secret, I began bracing myself— how? Why? When would we have to vacate the apartment? My wife's fears had to stem from similar past experiences. Her words, her conviction, couldn't have come from nothing.

That damned rat's breach—the final violation— happened in late 1992, two years after Kuwait's catastrophe when we'd fled to Jordan.

Earlier that year, the government had issued a decree requiring all vehicles entering from Kuwait—those bearing black license plates indicating Iraqi registration from Kuwait Province—to either clear customs or surrender ownership if the owner couldn't afford the import fees. The deadline for compliance was set for 1992, leaving no room for negotiation. Given my circumstances at the time, I had no choice but to relinquish my car—a bitter surrender under the weight of forces beyond my control.

The decision to relinquish my car was agonizing— like abandoning a member of my own family. Yet I had no choice. At the time, I was still bound by Green Card procedures, and even if I'd had the means to pay the customs fees, circumstances forced me to surrender the car to my brother, Mahmoud Al Hamad. He had been a teacher in Kuwait at Abu Halifa School during the grim years of occupation and liberation, only to return broken—financially ruined, exhausted, and in a pitiable state. This was four months after Iraqi forces were expelled. Back in Jordan, he began teaching in Tabarbour, but soon requested a transfer to a remote rural area to cut living costs. His plea was granted, and he was relocated to Al-Faisaliyah School, south of Sahab. How could I demand payment from him in such wretched straits? Even if I were in dire need myself.

My morale plummeted after losing my car—an involuntary loss that shackled my freedom and stripped away the simple luxury of going wherever I pleased. For the first time, I felt the crushing futility of clinging to a job whose wages couldn't even cover basic expenses. Resentment festered as I grappled with the injustice of my meager salary, though I still loved the work itself. Whispers of doubt crept in: The company's exploiting me. They knew my hands were tied by the green card's constraints—knew I couldn't maneuver, quit, or even demand a raise like my colleagues. That invisible chain, one I'd fought to break since returning from Kuwait, still held me fast. Time and again, I'd tried to reclaim my right to the yellow card, but hope slipped through my fingers like sand. By then, the aftershocks of the crisis had begun to etch themselves visibly onto my father in law. Jobless, his sole attempt at running a vegetable stall had collapsed spectacularly, hastened by the day his son Abdullah nearly lost his fingers to a banana-harvesting knife. His chain-smoking grew ravenous, his isolation thickened, and the shadows of depression clung to him. When his health deteriorated, doctors diagnosed blocked arteries in his lower body, prescribing walking to stimulate the dormant vessels in his legs.

I remember one evening when he asked me to join his therapeutic stroll around the neighborhood. Midway, his foot caught on a pebble—no larger than a pistachio—and the once-stalwart athlete crumpled to the ground like a stumbling child. I scrambled to gather his shattered pride, his headscarf, as I helped him rise. To this day, I don't know why they never operated to clear that early-diagnosed blockage—the very thing that would later kill him. Was it for medical reasons? Or, as I suspect, simply because he couldn't afford it?

I would often consult my wife and her father, along with a handful of close friends, about the suffocating predicament that bound me. The situation grew even more pressing as my eldest son, Ahmed, reached the age for kindergarten and school—yet once again, the labyrinth of green card restrictions barred him from enrolling in public schools. After months of anguish, and upon the advice of friends and consultations with the relevant department at the Ministry of Foreign Affairs, I finally arrived at a solution: traveling to the West Bank to file a family reunification application for my wife. The cruel irony was that I wanted the application rejected—because only then could I secure permanent residency in Jordan.

The thought of leaving Jordan and my job under such circumstances was terrifying. My wife, surrounded by her large family—who, like us, had been displaced from Kuwait—adamantly refused the idea. But as our legal limbo tightened its grip, strangling every aspect of our lives and leaving us no room to maneuver, I resolved to proceed with the application. Perhaps, if fate intervened, our residency woes would finally end.

The gravest fear we harbored was an approval for family reunification instead of a rejection. If granted, it would force us—amidst dire financial straits—to leave Jordan and remain in the West Bank for at least a year, as stipulated by reunification requirements. In practice, this meant embarking on a renewed journey of displacement, returning to square one, back to the very struggle of finding work and shelter in the grip of a crushing financial crisis. We barely had enough for travel expenses.

Worse still, returning would mean abandoning the job that provided our bare necessities. But the bitterest pill to swallow was the looming possibility that I might have to return to construction work in Palestine—the very work I had reluctantly taken up after high school, my first taste of backbreaking toil. The memory of that time remains raw and searing, a wound unhealed despite half a century passing. I doubt it will ever fade.

Red, Yellow, Green

Thus, in a desperate bid to escape our precarious existence—to break free from the knife-edge balance of survival and secure permanent residency in Jordan—the gates of opportunity creaked open for me and my family. With all other options exhausted, I made the fateful decision to travel to the West Bank to file for family reunification with my wife. We clung to the whispered promise that rejection was certain—a rejection we could leverage for permanent status. Never did my wife and I imagine settling there at that stage. The reasons were plain: we owned not a sliver of wealth, had no home, no stable income, no means to sustain life. I knew all too well the stifling scarcity of opportunities there, the crushing weight of unbearable living costs. We would likely suffer immensely, especially in the transition period before finding work.

As my mentor and friend Al-Natsha used to say, "Wishes won't wash dishes"—so how then could we build a home from nothing? The gold trinkets we'd been selling to survive were nearly gone. Clinging to my meager job at the General Products Company became our only lifeline—a grudging acceptance of our hand-to-mouth existence until some brighter path revealed itself.

I began steeling myself for the journey, though the familiar restlessness and pre-travel melancholy crept in. If voluntary travel is but a fragment of torment, as mentioned in the Hadith, then constrained passage across bridges becomes torment incarnate. Whenever I contemplated crossing to the West Bank, my mind conjured the image of that old man from one of my earlier journeys—how he had grabbed his headscarf and rushed out barefoot, forgetting his shoes at the physical security checkpoint. The shouts still echoed in my memory—" You there—old man! You forgot your shoes!" This was during my first crossing in the early 1970s.

After days of deliberation—of back-and-forth discussions, of resolve wavering like a candle in the wind—I finally made my decision. My wife, though reluctant to be uprooted from her comfort, her family's warm embrace, had softened after I reassured her of my intentions. And so, I resolved to move forward, securing a leave of absence from the company for a few days and embarked on the journey, bracing myself for the ordeal of travel—an ordeal that began the moment I crossed the iron gate.

The first station was stepping off the bus for inspection. Then came the baggage checkpoint for screening, followed by the identity verification window, where cryptic letters in some coded language were stamped on the cover—likely carrying messages for those seated behind the counter inside. Next was the physical search, then the entry stamp, with the added possibility of being hosted by what they called the Public Relations Department. Finally, retrieving my luggage and exiting the hall—unless, of course, there was a manual bag search or an involuntary detainment at customs.

I remember that journey—if my memory serves me right—as the first time I experienced it. They'd make you pass through a physical inspection area, a cramped room no larger than a prison cell. The moment you stepped inside, the psychological expert stationed there would press a button, triggering a light signal mounted within the room—the same kind found at street intersections. The colors would then flicker aggressively, accompanied by an irritating, jarring tune. Red, yellow, green—they flashed chaotically before settling on a single hue. I believe it was always red. The purpose, it seemed, was to test the newcomer's reaction to the sudden appearance of danger, to provoke hidden truths, if any existed.

I turned my face away the instant the machine lit up, refusing to let the strobing colors manipulate my expressions or stir my emotions. I crossed safely to the other side, yet remnants of that experience clung to me, leaving behind a shadow of unease that lingers still, as if waiting for the Day of Resurrection.

I encountered no problems during the baggage inspection - I'm scrupulously observant about never carrying prohibited items listed in the bridge crossing notices. This careful compliance helps me avoid any hurdles that might cause what we call 'red-tape hassles,' unnecessary delays, or customs fines.

At long last, the moment of deliverance arrived. I made my way to the red bus that ferried passengers to Jericho, quietly reciting the Shahada as I always did upon emerging from those stations of palpable torment. I traveled via the Bridge cars to my village, Kifl Haris, and finally arrived at the family home. The house was now occupied by my brother Ahmed's family—he who had cared for our father during his illness. Were it not for the presence of my aunt, the mother who replaced my own after my biological mother's passing in my early childhood, I would have been crushed by a desolate estrangement. This was, after all, the first time I had entered the family home since my father's passing—since his absence. May God have mercy on him. But my aunt's presence softened the crisis within me, wrapping me in the solace of stability and the warmth of familial embrace.

Later—unusually for a Palestinian village—very few people came to welcome me after my long absence. I might not have noticed this at all had it not been for my uncle, Abdulhamid Odah. He was an elderly, wise man who, long before lawyers became commonplace in the region, served as the village's de facto legal counsel. People sought him out to draft petitions, contracts, and agreements, all written in his impeccably formal, legally precise language. That day, he had come to greet me, and we sat together in the courtyard under the mulberry tree, exchanging light conversation. Then, abruptly, he said:

"Do you realize, Khalil, had we heard before your arrival that you were coming with a fortune in a money sack, we'd have come in seven stretch limousines to welcome you at the bridge? But since word reached us that you'd be arriving empty-handed, don't expect anyone to come greet you."

And my uncle, Abu Mohammed, spoke the truth—confirming the popular saying that a man's worth in the eyes of others depends on the weight of his purse. As the proverb goes: "You are what you own" to the world, but without money, you are nothing—even if you are a guru or the wisest of sages.

The next day, after seeking counsel from others, the time came to submit my family reunification request. I went to the Civil Administration headquarters in Salfit, filled out the application according to protocol, and waited in the compound's courtyard until I was summoned for an interview.

The officer—apparently intrigued by my profession listed as "Translator" in the passport—paused, studying me. "Your work," he began, "your studies... Which university did you graduate from?"

So I replied:

I'm a graduate of San Diego State University in California, USA, with a master's degree in English Literature. I spoke to him in fluent English—and to my surprise, he responded with equal fluency. He told me he had studied at the same university. And just like that, the interview ended without further questions.

Studying in Yankee Land— a decision that would plunge my family and me into a terrible predicament. We would have no choice but to follow through, or else we would find ourselves in dire straits. As the saying goes: "Neither here nor there." And if we went through with it and exhausted our means, we would inevitably be hurling ourselves into ruin. I would have to abandon a stable job, a steady income that covered our basic needs, and a life of quiet contentment—modest as it was—free from major hardships. Instead, we would enter a vast prison of darkness upon darkness, a phase shrouded in uncertainty, with pessimism as its defining mark.

The following day, I returned to my family and my work in Amman. We began waiting—watching, holding our breath—for the military governor's decision regarding our reunification papers. Outwardly, we carried on as if we were staying, preparing ourselves for rejection. But inwardly, a silent dread took root: what if the mouse had already sniffed out our imminent departure? If so, approval was inevitable, and we stood on the precipice of a crushing new reality—a chapter of hardship that would eclipse all we'd endured thus far. This would be the cruelest stretch, the most unrelenting, a time that made us at sixes and sevens—when every past misery would pale like a prelude, and the true dance of suffering had yet to begin.

Winds Blow Counter
to what Ships Desire

I returned to the eastern bank of the river after submitting the family reunification papers for my wife, throwing myself back into work at the General Products Trading Company while waiting for news from our family on the western bank. In truth, my wife and I secretly hoped for a rejection—permanent residency would solve many of our problems, sparing us from being uprooted again in less than three years. After our forced and catastrophic expulsion from Kuwait, we had finally found some stability in Amman. No one could endure another upheaval so sudden, especially with our finances reduced to nothing. If the approval came and we were compelled to comply, we would undoubtedly plunge into a tunnel of misery, hardship, and destitution.

Since reunification approvals often took years, we didn't expect an answer so soon. So we put the matter behind us, trying to reclaim some semblance of routine, forcing our eyes forward. Yet in such circumstances, no matter how hard you try, you can't ignore an impending event that might tear you from your fragile comfort and turn your life upside down. Worse, we feared it would drag us into pitch-black corridors—especially after a wretched rat had invaded our once-safe home. My wife saw it as an unmistakable omen, an early warning, a foreshadowing message from the intruder foretelling departure.

But our waiting was not long. After only a few months—perhaps three or four—the winds shifted against our wishes. News came that our names had been approved for family reunification. Then came the moment of truth, leaving us in a quandary—whether to seize this precarious opportunity or ignore it, though ignoring it carried grave risks. Foremost among these was losing all claim to identity and residency rights in the West Bank for my wife.

The truth was, we had no choice but to leave everything behind and leave in haste—even if we were down to our last penny—just to cross the border before our entry permit expired. Otherwise, we would lose our right to family reunification forever, leaving us adrift: neither me here, nor my wife there, and the future of our children hanging by a thread.

My wife had no choice but to reluctantly surrender to this harsh new reality. I believe the memory of that mouse invading our home months earlier - how she'd shuddered at its presence - played no small part in her reluctant acceptance. It helped push her to tear herself away from the familial warmth she cherished, from the place she loved, and follow me into this new tunnel of exile and displacement - one that promised only deeper misery and hardship, despite the tremors of fear she felt about embarking on such an uncertain journey.

We dismantled our home in haste, stacking our belongings in the storage room of her uncle Nabil Shakhtour. We clung to the fragile hope that one day—once the mandatory detention period for obtaining residency papers ended—we'd return to reclaim them. The apartment was handed back to the landlord, though a fraction of the unpaid rent still weighed on our conscience. I severed ties with the company where I had worked, and together we carried only what our hands could hold. Our departure was a race against the clock: we left in the final hours, mere days before our entry permit expired—a breathless escape with our future crumpled in our pockets.

We had boarded the airport shuttle from outside the home of my father-in-law, in Bayader Wadi Al-Seer, amid deafening wails and torrents of tears from my wife, her mother, and the relatives who had gathered to bid us farewell. It was as though we were being marched to certain doom.

We surely tasted bitterness twice over on that bridge-crossing journey. If travel under ordinary circumstances is a slice of torment for a lone wayfarer—light of baggage and spirit—then imagine the agony of a family traveling with small children and heavy belongings, scorched by the anguish of leaving loved ones behind. They depart their place of comfort, reluctantly yet resolutely, knowing they leap into a frying pan of fire, trembling at the calamities they dread and strive to avoid. In such moments, the miller's day stretches not merely to one day as the saying goes, but to an endless month—its sunlit hours and lightless nights alike.

Our arrival in Kifl Haris marked the start of a new chapter for my small family and me—one written in the ink of fresh sorrow. With no other choice, we turned to the home of my eldest brother Ahmed, a modest house of two newly built concrete-and-brick rooms flanking an ancient clay archway. The archway's room, its ceiling sagging like a weary back, seemed one gust away from collapse.

Then there was the toilet—the demons' den—an outhouse at the far end of the garden. Venturing there at night was an ordeal of its own, a tale woven with terrors: darkness, scorpions, snakes, jinn, hyenas, and devils all played their part. And so, as children, we became pioneers in "recycling" empty ghee cans, repurposing them as chamber pots. We kept them inside the room at night to avoid the deadly risks lurking outside especially the touch of the jinn, the first boogeyman in the shadowed nights of the countryside.

This was the state of our family home—the very place where we grew up—even though my brother Ahmed had been working in construction since being unjustly forced out of school in the sixth grade. The education system in the 1950s barred students from continuing their studies if they exceeded a certain age when advancing to the next grade. Yet over the years, he became a skilled master builder, participating in the construction of tens of thousands of villas, apartment buildings, and structures, many in Palestinian territories and some towering high in the coastal city of Herzliya, where I worked alongside him for several months right after my high school exams. Our situation perfectly embodied the old saying: "The shoemaker's wife is always the worst shod."

This brother had been the family's primary provider, earning his living through the sweat of his brow all his life. Like the rest of our brothers, he eventually made his way to Kuwait for work. Yet unlike them, he returned and took care for our father when he fell victim to a stroke, leaving him paralyzed. With patience and resignation, he tended to our father throughout his illness, which stretched on for years. Meanwhile, we, the other siblings, remained far from the scene of that deeply painful ordeal—still in Kuwait.

In those early days after our return, we crowded with a handful of my brother Ahmed's children in one of the three cramped rooms with my aunt Halwa Al-Asaad's house, her joy at having us there brighter than her name. At night, we would spread out on the floor to sleep, lining up side by side, pressed together like sardines in a tin. By day, we passed our time in the courtyard, under the shade of the mulberry tree, or in the surrounding gardens, and in my brother Hamad's adjacent house.

While our children lost themselves in the freedom of open spaces—playing folk games, chasing rabbits, chickens, and cats through the countryside— I found myself drowning in the sweetness of returning to the place where I was born. This was the land that shaped my childhood, where every corner overflowed with golden memories and the rich perfume of the past.

How could it be otherwise? When you sit in the courtyard's heart, beautiful memories come rushing back. There, my father used to sit, pressing the honeycomb between his fingers. Over there, we would light the fire in the brazier. On this branch of the mulberry tree, we tied the swing's rope. And in that corner, we tethered the black-and-white spotted cow—we called her the Honeyed One, for her gentleness. Meanwhile, the red-and-white spotted cow was tied farther away, near the donkey's trough. We never gave her a name; we just called her the Red Cow—for her ferocity.

As for my wife—born in Kuwait, accustomed to apartment living all her life —she must have felt a double alienation: that of place and that of people. Yet she never showed any struggle to adapt to her new surroundings. Instead, she soon blended into the rhythm of life, harmonizing with my family and relatives as if she were a daughter of the countryside herself. Later, she even joined my brother's family in gathering olives.

Days passed, and we remained in that wretched, miserable state—stuck in place, with no way forward. Had it not been for my aunt's kindness, there would have been no room for us at all, and my brother Ahmed and his family would never have endured our presence for so long. Never mind that this was the family home, which, by tradition, should have passed to the youngest son after our father's death—me.

No doubt he tolerated our presence reluctantly. The moment I asked to borrow some money, he first instructed me to find myself a place to live, then informed me he only had 450 dinars to his name. He told me he would give me the money on one condition—that I never ask him for help again.

Truth be told, his refusal struck me like a blow. If this was how my own brother —my flesh and blood— would treat me, refusing to lend me money to ease my hardship and pull me out of my distress, even though he knew full well my circumstances and the state of my family, then who could I turn to? He was well-off, his finances soaring high—so what did it cost him to help?

Yet I couldn't bring myself to resent him, not even in the face of such coldness. He had done too much for our family, sacrificed too much. For years, he had cared for our father, and after his death, he took on the burden of looking after our aunt—while the rest of us siblings lived our own comfortable lives in Kuwait, far removed from the pain my father endured.

To Lose a Mother and Father
Is to Lose the Hands That Held You

The moment my struggling, beloved brother asked me to find us a place to live, the world—vast as it was—seemed to close in around me. There was no longer room for my family and me in that house, and I had no choice but to urgently find shelter, even if it meant pitching a tent on a threshing floor. Truth be told, those first days after our arrival were spent on the fringes of life in the family home. Staying there was a kind of madness—an impossible, degrading existence that, if prolonged, threatened to unravel our minds and bodies. Even rats, when crammed into a cage, develop high blood pressure and sickness. And our conditions are unbearable, unlivable, the space too tight, too crowded.

So, without argument, without demanding my inheritance or my rightful place in the family home, I simply began searching for somewhere to rent. There would be no arguing with a man who had devoted his life to serving and providing for his family. Let him do as he pleased; in my eyes, he was absolved, like the warriors of Badr.

Thankfully, my search for a home did not last long. Word reached me that my eldest uncle, Ahmed Al-Asaad, had a separate apartment on the second floor and was looking to rent it out. I hurried to him at once—for as the saying goes, "A maternal uncle is a second father," a truth known all too well by those orphaned early in life, when a mother leans on her brother's shoulder and on no one else's. In such times, the uncle becomes the father, bound by the same blood as the mother. And this uncle, in particular, was an extraordinary man—truly exceptional. He possessed a musical voice, so tender and melancholic, that we would hum along, enchanted by its beauty as he recited the Quran, chanting its verses with melodic precision. He was among those who will be resurrected on the Day of Judgment with elongated necks, for he was a muezzin whose voice carried a profound resonance, stirring the souls of all who heard it. When he proclaimed 'Allah is the Greatest,' its power was such that even trees and stones might have trembled, so mesmerizing was his call to prayer.

I felt my wife and children would be safe within the walls of his large house during my absence. Surely he would treat us with a father's tenderness. For this assurance, I was prepared to pay whatever rent he demanded without question—despite my strained circumstances—without even inspecting the apartment beforehand.

When I asked about the rent, he named his price: seventy-five Jordanian dinars a month. A staggering sum for a modest apartment in the Palestinian countryside at that time. And it was unfurnished, too—nothing but a battered gas stove, no oven, the kind used by lonely bachelors in foreign lands. The path to his house was paved with broken tombstones. His home stood in the northern part of our village, Kifl Haris, just meters from the graveyard where the dead were buried. Ancient graves surrounded it on all sides, and the only way to reach it was by walking over the remnants of old tombs, their markers still faintly visible. These graves stand as silent witnesses to the ancient roots of the village, whose soil cradles the tombs and shrines of prophets—among them Dhul-Kifl and Dhul-Nun. At its heart lies the shrine of Prophet Yusha, surrounded by an old burial ground stretching all the way to the modern cemetery. This means that to reach my uncle's house in the center of town, you must walk over graves, through the remnants of an old cemetery—though its markers and headstones have nearly vanished. Time has paved an asphalt road cuts through its heart, and school buildings now stand on vast stretches of it.

Though stunned by the exorbitant fare and filled with silent disbelief, I swallowed my anger along with my pride, nodding agreement under the pressing need to escape my brother's house—the so-called "family home." My own family desperately needed liberation from that sardine tin of a room, the cramped space we'd shared with my aunt ever since our arrival from the East Bank. Never mind that our Jordanian apartment—located in Bayader Wadi Al-Seer, one of West Amman's affluent districts—had cost no more than ninety dinars in rent.

I paid the rent in advance, as I continued to do punctually on the first of every month. Then came the task of gathering bedding and essential furniture. We acquired some old mattresses from the family house—relics, they told us, from my brother Mahmoud's wedding, celebrated in the village over twenty years earlier. We brought our clothes with us, but without a wardrobe, most of them remained imprisoned in suitcases or strewn across the floor around them. For years, until we finally left Kifl Haris, those suitcases sat in a corner of the bedroom, a room so bare it held no beds. We slept on the floor. As for the story of our departure from Kifl Haris to the city—that is a tale of drama and stirring detail, one I will share with you, God willing, in due course.

At long last, we emerged from that cramped cellar into a dwelling of our own. Beneath its roof we finally slept with some semblance of peace, though the place remained scarcely furnished with only the barest essentials. This modest refuge would have been beyond our reach had it not been for the dwindling remnants of gold pieces we still possessed - most of which we'd already sold. Even my brother Ahmed's loan of 450 dinars wouldn't have sufficed to establish this new home in a new land.

Driven by necessity, I turned again to my brother to borrow more money. I resolved to spare myself the humiliation of begging from anyone else—whether stranger or kin—save for my own flesh and blood. I knew all too well what their answers would be. The scars of Kuwait's ruin and the horrors that followed had taught me how quickly people abandon one another when crisis strikes.

This time, when I asked him for another loan, I said, "You're all I have in this world, brother." He told me he had no money to spare—and perhaps there was some truth to his words. He had recently purchased two plots of land, which must have cost him a fortune. And then there was the irregular heartbeat that had struck him earlier, leaving its mark not just on his health but on his very nature. It made him more cautious, and more fearful for his children's future. When a man believes death is near—when sickness whispers its arrival—something shifts inside him. Pity and sorrow for his family take root. He begins to act on instinct, as though every gesture is a farewell. He grows afraid for their fate, for what lies ahead, and in that fear, he wishes he could gather the whole world and everything in it—just to leave it all for them.

Instead of offering cash, he proposed I sell the honey from his harvest that season— midway through 1993. Rumor had it that my brother was feeding the bees sugar, and people took it as truth. The honey wouldn't sell, despite it being a good season. So, I was left to market nearly 300 kilograms of mountain honey. We agreed on my payment: two kilograms of honey for every ten I sold on his behalf.

And so I embarked on that difficult task—one that bordered on the impossible. For nothing is harder than selling honey. The dishonest swindlers had left no room for honest folk to be believed. Selling honey had become harder than peddling insurance policies, or trying to carry coal to Newcastle.

As for the execution, the task itself was not difficult. My aunt had trained me in the art of selling when I was just a child, sending me out to sell mulberries on a tray. Soon, I was carrying five kilos of honey in each hand, the weight straining the handles of those plastic baskets—ubiquitous in those days, perforated and splashed with garish yellows, greens, and reds. I would trek from village to town on foot, but the real ordeal lay in the baskets' handles— sharp as knife blades. Even when nearly empty, after a short while, you would feel your fingers were on the verge of snapping. Now imagine bearing ten kilos—five in each hand—marching for miles just to persuade a single soul to buy a single kilo of honey.

The truth is, there were times I would sell the entire batch in record time—no need for elaborate sales pitches about the honey's quality. This usually happened in places where people still remembered my late father, Abu Hamad, a man of good reputation, and his apiaries' sterling reputation.

Other days, I would struggle to sell even a single kilo, customers eyeing the jars with suspicion, fearing they might be adulterated. Some evenings, I would trudge home with every jar still in my satchel, living out that old saying: "You returned as you went."

One afternoon, after circling the streets of a nearby village trying in vain to sell the honey I carried, I found myself standing before the grand mosque at the town's center. It was just after the afternoon prayer, and I was still holding my jars of honey, unsold and heavy in my hands.

Suddenly, the owner of a grocery shop across from the mosque called out to me:
"Where're you from, uncle?"

"Kifl Haris," I replied.
"Do you know a fellow from your village—Farid Bouziya?"

"Know him?" I said. "I know him like my own brother."

The shopkeeper said: "Well, I go with your townsman here to the market. Every time, he buys ten crates of tomatoes, same for zucchini, cucumbers, and eggplant. Me? I just take this—" He jerked his chin toward a half-filled crate of tomatoes slumped in the corner of his shop.

Then he waved me off: "Go on, uncle. Take your honey and go. Don't waste your time in this town." The moment I heard the shopkeeper's words, I took the honey and came back to the house empty-handed. Yet I persisted, selling in other neighborhoods, pushing further each day until I reached distant areas—all the way to Jalamah in the north and Bethlehem in the south—after adding small straw trays to my wares.

Wherever I went, I began explaining to people at length about high-quality honey, the tools for testing its purity, and the ways it could be adulterated. Over time, I earned their trust and managed to sell the entire season's stock. Of course, I paid my brother the bulk of the earnings little by little. Once I had successfully completed the task, I gathered the papers where I had recorded the sales and payments and went to settle the account with him.

By the end of our meeting, we agreed that my debt to him stood at a mere 600 dinars—nothing more. After ensuring his satisfaction, I asked:
"Should I tear up the records?"
"Yes," he replied.
So I tore them apart.
If only I hadn't.

A Day of Sixes and Sevens

Once we had settled into our new life and secured a place of our own, my foremost concern became securing life's basic necessities—chief among them, infant formula and food. I had two young sons to care for, and we were expecting a third child, a daughter who would complete our fledgling family."

I began scouring old notebooks for anyone whose door I might knock on - someone who could stand by me during those desperate times. My search led me to my late friend Dr. Moeen Jaber, my former roommate in Bayt Sahur during our university years at Bethlehem University. He now ran a secondhand goods shop on Jerusalem Street in Balata Camp. I went to him and came away with a battered, rudimentary television set. Truth be told, I can no longer remember whether I also obtained other furnishings like chairs to make our house habitable. But what remains etched in memory is his generosity—the act of a noble man and cherished friend whose kindness I shall never forget. I cannot recall whether he ever asked me to pay for those items or simply gave them to me as a gift.

From my colleagues at Yusuf Ahmed Al-Ghanim's company in Kuwait was Mr. Labib Al-Zamil, from Deir Al-Hatab. After being forcibly expelled from Kuwait in the wake of the disaster that uprooted us from that oil-rich land, I learned he had opened a small shop across from the market. Somehow, I managed to track down the shop's location. When I went to see him, I was certain he wouldn't turn me away—and he didn't. The moment I asked if I could take a few supplies on credit, he opened not just his shop but his heart, urging me to take whatever I needed. True to his word, I left with essentials: milk, rice, sugar, salt, and other necessities for survival. Now, looking back, I can't recall whether I ever repaid him. Most likely, I simply couldn't afford to during those early days of our return.

Despite my utmost efforts to find work from the very moment I arrived—even if it meant laboring in construction, a job I had deeply despised in my youth and fled the country to avoid. Yet, even that was beyond my reach. Months passed after our return, and nothing.

And of course, I must have made the rounds of all the major companies and institutions in Nablus during that time, submitting job applications wherever I could. I mention this because later, I received an unexpected phone call that would change everything. The director of one of Nablus's most prominent companies offered me a position - though I couldn't even recall when I'd applied to them. In due course, as events unfolded, I'll share the story of that fateful call that rescued me from the depths of the aluminum factory where I was then trapped.

Seven Lean Years

Though the late Dr. Moeen Jaber and Mr. Labib Al-Zamil's support helped meet some basic needs and temporarily relieved the most pressing food and living crises, securing daily meals remained my greatest burden and foremost priority. I struggled tirelessly to put food on the table for my family. When funds ran desperately low, I turned to the wilderness, foraging for anything edible - wild pears, hawthorns, almonds, figs, olives, wild lettuce, mallow, and even truffles when season permitted.

It so happened that the skies opened in the rainy season of late 1993. By then, we'd spent months in my uncle's rented apartment, our financial crisis having plummeted to its nadir—especially after I discovered I owed my brother two thousand Jordanian dinars, not the six hundred I'd imagined. We could barely find anything to eat, and I was still unemployed. When whispers spread that the rains had brought truffle season, I was desperate to gather some myself from beneath the oak trees in the mountains surrounding Wadi Qana, in the lands near the village of Deir Istiya, close to our hometown, Kifl Haris. That oak-covered forest was at least four or five kilometers away. It wasn't just hunger that drove me, but the yearning to partake in that annual ritual, to feel the earth's generosity.

But I didn't own a proper pair of sneakers for the rough, mountainous terrain. So I turned to my uncle Ahmed's wife—that tender-hearted woman who always showed us kindness in every way, greeted us with smiles, and never ceased to speak fondly of my mother. She had, in many ways, filled the void of a mother's and grandmother's warmth. I asked her if they had any boots I could wear for my trip to the mountains to hunt truffles.

My uncle's wife gave me an old, worn-out pair of shoes from their storage room to wear. After inspecting them, I was certain they were unfit for such a journey—not across this rugged, thorn-scattered mountain terrain, especially damp from recent rains. But with hunger gnawing at us and the fierce desire to join the communal truffle harvest— a ritual that drew crowds of eager foragers—I had no other choice. With no alternative, I slipped them on and set out on foot toward Wadi Qana. My path wound through olive groves, across open wilderness, past the barren slopes of Al-Rama Al-Shami, then onward through the Dhahr Al-Iraq highlands until I reached the truffle-rich mountains of Wadi Qana. There, after the skies roared with thunder and the earth drank its fill of rain, the truffles would emerge in abundance—a season of plenty.

I wandered deeper among the oak trees on the mountainside flanking the asphalt road that cut through the valley toward Jinsafut, then onward to Nablus and Qalqilya. Eventually, I found a few truffles—but my search was cut short when the sole of my worn-out shoe tore clean off, leaving me half-barefoot. My left foot tread unprotected while the right still clung to its tattered covering. Most of my path was strewn with thorns, mud, and jagged stones. After futile attempts to repair the shoe, I tied a black plastic bag around my left foot, a hopeless shield against the brambles. It frayed within moments, forcing me to trek back—across valleys, up the mountain, the entire distance to my village, Kifl Haris—with one foot bare and the other nearly so.

That journey tested me to my limits. I saw noonday stars—so brutal was the path that not a single spot on my feet remained unscathed by thorns or bruises. I've kept the secret of this bitter ordeal locked away, never speaking of what happened during that trek to anyone—not even my wife. She endured every hardship we faced, adapting to the cruelest conditions of our wretched existence without complaint. Yet one thing she could neither accept nor comprehend: living among graves. For her, this became a waking nightmare.

As for vegetables, during my frequent visits to my cousin's son, Dr. Karam, at his pharmacy near the Salfit junction—a place I often went to, where we would sit and chat under the Storax tree—I noticed that my other cousin's son, Saleh, who owned a vegetable stall nearby, would discard large quantities of produce at the slightest sign of bruising or rot. They would later end up in the garbage bins. I, however, often salvaged what I could, taking some home under the pretense that it was a sin to throw away "perfectly good food." The truth, of course, was that I couldn't afford to buy vegetables. This free produce became a crucial part of our survival, easing the burden of our expenses.

These pitch-black circumstances persisted for several more months, while the misery, poverty, and grinding hardship continued for years—though faint glimmers of hope flickered here and there. In time, I'll recount every detail of those wretched days for you.

A Fracture in Misery's Wall

As mentioned earlier, the initial period after our arrival from Amman to our village, Kifl Haris— meant for family reunification—was exceedingly difficult. This catastrophic phase lasted over six months, during which we endured unbearable hardships, and I relentlessly searched for work, even in construction—a field I had worked in before and despised. But securing my family's basic needs for food, drink, and clothing took precedence.

During that time, I often wandered the village streets, adrift in emptiness and the idleness of unemployment. Yet I never surrendered to poverty. Soon, I began selling straw trays after exhausting my brother's entire honey harvest for the year—a decision that ultimately buried me under a debt of two thousand Jordanian dinars, tightening the noose of financial hardship around my neck.

I began focusing on selling small handmade straw crafts produced by village women—items easily carried in plastic or burlap sacks slung across my shoulders. With my wares in tow, I wandered through nearby hamlets and distant, forgotten corners of the land. My journeys sometimes took me as far as Jalamah, north of Jenin near Nazareth, where shopfronts glittered like some garish carnival, all catering to the Arabs inside the Green

Line—those coming through the checkpoint erected near the so-called "Green Line."

Once, after selling a relatively large load of trays in Al-Jalama—with a decent profit after accounting for travel and expenses—I decided to celebrate this small triumph. And so I did: upon returning to Nablus, I bought myself a shawarma sandwich. The taste of that meat, tucked into bread like a gift from heaven, was unforgettable, almost mythical.

And as one thing leads to another—one day, as I strolled down from the town center toward Al-Safra junction, right in front of Abu Al-Munjed's house, I spotted a damp banknote on the ground. It was a fifty-shekel bill, soaked by rain and runoff from a nearby drain. I picked it up with swift, tender joy, hiding it quickly lest anyone see. Back home, my wife and I dried it carefully over the gas stove, then hung it on the clothesline to crisp up in the air. With that money, I bought two chickens, and my wife cooked a feast so delicious that the taste of that chicken was extraordinary—a flavor etched forever in memory.

On one occasion, I was wandering aimlessly through the alleyway—perhaps on my way to my sister Aisha's house near the Nabi Kifl area. My path took me through the heart of the neighborhood, past the guesthouse, then through the eastern alley where my sister lived. That day, I was wearing a gray djellaba with thin black stripes. As I passed by

Nawaf Al-Tabsh's house, I happened upon a group of women standing in a circle in the middle of the street, whispering among themselves. Among them, I recognized our relative Amina al-Sharif. I paid them no mind whatsoever and continued on my way, never imagining that I would become the object of their gossip and mockery in that moment. But days later, when I visited Aisha again, the truth surfaced. There, I met Amina Al-Sherif—my brother-in-law's sister—who informed me that those women had indeed ridiculed me. She asked me, with a knowing smile, when we met:

"Khalil, do you know what those women said about you the other day when you walked past us in the alley?"

"No," I replied. "Only God knows what's in people's hearts."

She said, "They mocked you, saying, 'Look at this fool—what is he even wearing?!' Their fingers gestured at the djellaba you had on."

The truth is, I was stunned by what I heard. Inside, I thought: What silly matters do they care about?! But I came to understand those women's perspectives well enough. Neither they nor anyone else could know the turmoil inside me—the pain, loneliness, alienation, the grinding poverty, the constant weight of debt, and the financial strain. These harsh realities had made clothing, like all personal matters, secondary concerns for me. Besides, for those who work in the Gulf, wearing a djellaba eventually becomes second nature, something you barely think about. Yet to those raised in the world of trousers and button-down shirts, it remains alien—even if the djellaba were woven from the finest silk.

I remembered how the woman—the supervisor of the dormitory where I lived in one of its apartments in America—had recoiled in shock when Umm Kulthum's songs filled the room, songs I had been listening to with sheer delight. To her, it sounded like funeral music and, with a grimace of disgust, she demanded I turn off the tape recorder.

Despite my brisk trade in selling trays, our financial situation remained dire during that period. When we needed a kerosene heater to ward off the cold, I went to Engineer Arafat Saleh Al-Arif—grandson of the legendary Aref Al-Aref, the very man who played a pivotal role in my return from the United States. This Arafat had recently opened a small shop in a storage room attached to Jasser family's property. I bought the heater from him on credit, of course. Sadly, he was forced to shutter the shop soon after. Like so many village merchants, he found himself drowning in unpaid customer debts. In the end, he chose the stability of a salaried job rather than continue selling on tab—preferring, as the saying goes, "Slow and steady wins the race."

As the due date for my daughter Shurooq's birth approached in late May 1994, money was tight. When the time came, I took my wife to the maternity ward at Rafidia Government Hospital in Nablus—despite the whispers we had heard about neglected care. Shurooq would be the only one of my children born in a public hospital, a concession to our empty pockets that year, which couldn't stretch to cover a private hospital's fees. Yet against all fears, everything unfolded beautifully there, with the medical staff demonstrating remarkable competence.

We rejoiced at the birth of Shurooq and her arrival into our small family. As the saying goes, 'A daughter brings blessings with her,' which is why we named her Shurooq—both because she was fair-haired from birth, and in hopes she would prove auspicious for us, that our days might brighten with prosperity. Perhaps through her, we would emerge from the long night of poverty that had darkened our lives for so long.

Truth be told, it wasn't long after that when Mr. Hani Daoud reached out to me. Though we had never met before, he was from the neighboring village of Haris, just next to ours. By profession, he was a schoolteacher—but he also worked as a labor contractor, supplying workers for some of the factories in Burgan's industrial area, which stood on Haris's land. He offered me a job at an aluminum factory in that industrial area. Of course, I accepted immediately, even though I had no idea about what the work entailed or who'd told him I was looking for employment.

Before I set foot in that factory, whispers of its brutality had reached me. Yet the reality proved far worse than anything I had been told. It was more like a labor camp than a factory, all because of the relentless production cycle. In time, I will lay bare the particulars of my suffering there, stitch by stitch. But for all its cruelty, this job became a single thread of light slipped through the wall of misery and poverty that had trapped me for so long.

Five Months in the Depths
of the Aluminum Factory

I was overjoyed to receive the job offer at the aluminum factory in Burgan industrial area, near our village of Kifl Haris. The income was desperately needed—for me, for my family. Despite my profound aversion to labor in such places, both on principle and from a previous bitter experience. Work of this sort demands no mental effort or academic qualifications—just immense patience, endurance, and raw physical strength. It was labor equally suited to the university graduate and the school dropout, the kind of grueling, mind-numbing toil often dismissed as mere "donkey work."

I headed to the meeting point I had agreed upon with Mr. Hani Daoud, the labor contractor, and headed to the Safra Junction near Ismail Al-Radi's house at the edge of town. It was a spot where clusters of young men from the town would gather, those who worked at the same factory or other workshops nearby.

I arrived just as the sun rose. Soon after, Mr. Hani appeared at the exact spot and drove us to the factory in his car. There, he spoke privately with the Arab manager from Gaza—a towering man, solidly built, with the commanding presence of a leadership and charisma. He was from Gaza City, and they called him Mahmoud Al-Ghazawi. He approached me, leaned in, and confided that he had personally vouched for me to the manager. "He knows you are an educated man," he whispered, "that you hold an advanced degree. I made sure he wouldn't assign you any degrading work." At that moment, I had no idea what infamous task he meant.

I thanked him warmly and hurried back to join the other workers before they noticed our whispered exchange—before their suspicions could flare.

The first thing I did when I started work at that factory was pick up a broom I found lying on the floor and begin to sweep. My intention was to send a clear message to the workers who knew me: I was one of them. I had come to labor alongside them, shedding the aura of the educated man—the holder of degrees, the veteran of white-collar jobs in Kuwait's and Jordan's corporate giants. Under that factory's roof, my diplomas would grant me no special status from any other man there.

I was the only worker in the factory with a master's degree—a graduate of an American university, no less. Later, Mr. Dhuqan Al-Qayshawi joined the workforce, holding a bachelor's degree in computer systems. Suddenly, we were two educated men among the laborers, making us two educated employees in a sea of men who had either dropped out of school before even reaching the general secondary certificate 'Tawjihi,' or else they abandoned education altogether after high school.

It later became clear that the factory work was monotonous in nature. The task consisted of hanging ready-made aluminum profiles onto a moving rail that ran along the factory ceiling, roughly two meters above the ground. In Hebrew, they called it a 'sharsheret'—a chain. From it dangled iron plates with drilled holes, and the workers, who had to operate in pairs, were required to hang the profiles meant for painting before they reached the painting furnace. They had to mount the aluminum profiles using thin bolts, inserting them into the narrow holes of the swaying plates. This meant the worker had to remain in a state of constant alertness, in perpetual motion, as he and his partner carried the aluminum profile to hang it before the rail rushed past—swift as a cloud. A man could barely keep up.

This meant the job required two workers in tandem—each gripping one end of an aluminum profile, lifting it, and hooking it onto iron bolts. They had to carefully slot the profiles into holes drilled into the plates descending from the conveyor, securing them in place before the assembly traveled toward the furnace. As the profiles rotated inside, they would be coated with the color specified for each order. Once painted, the workers would remove them from the conveyor, load fresh profiles, and repeat the cycle. All of it had to be done at breakneck speed, without pause or fatigue, striving to hang five or six profiles in the mounting zone each time—before the conveyor rumbled onward to the furnace, where the chosen color would be baked onto the metal.

And imagine, if you will, the sheer difficulty of this labor; for the worker is constrained by the relentless, automated movement of the rapid conveyor system on one hand, while on the other, he must move in perfect synchrony with his partner to lift the profiles destined for painting. These come in various shapes and weights—some reaching up to twenty-five kilograms—only to then collaboratively hang them upon an exceedingly slender nail within a narrow opening, on thin panels suspended from a moving track. Neither may pass through the furnace without being properly prepared with its required coating, for to do so would be to waste both paint and precious time.

The truth was, hanging those profiles at such speed, in that manner, under near-impossible conditions, was grueling—exhausting to the point of numbness. I remember returning home each night utterly broken by exhaustion after eight relentless hours. The fatigue would multiply when we were forced into overtime, which happened more often than not. Or when your work partner happened to be slow-moving, or short-statured, or weak-eyed—requiring extra minutes to locate those narrow holes where we hammered in the bolts to hang the profiles. What was already backbreaking labor would then become torture magnified tenfold. There were days when I could barely manage the walk back to my lodges after the car dropped us off at the fork of Al-Safra at the town's entrance. From there, I had to trek the remaining distance—up the ascending path of Nabi Kifl, then through Al-Rama Al-Shami, a kilometer or more of weary steps.

Personally, I always pitied one particular worker— a short-statured man with poor eyesight and a difficult disposition. Yet his desperate need to support his family was evident. While other laborers avoided him, I, in my idealism, would volunteer to work alongside him. Not because anyone asked me to, nor to make him feel indebted to my exhausting charity. And that, in turn, drained me with an exhaustion beyond bearing.

Yet despite the grueling labor—the backbreaking effort, the scarcity of time, the relentless pace of our duties—we still sifted golden specks of daylight. Laughter bubbled up between exhaustion, Quranic verses hummed like a soothing chant, and debates flared like sparks in the dark, lively and bright. The work environment—and the bonds between the laborers—was warm and beautiful.

The first grueling month at the factory came to an end, and I received a generous paycheck—over three thousand shekels, thanks to overtime. When I returned home, I asked my wife and young children to gather before me. I climbed onto a chair like a man about to deliver a speech, then pulled out the cash I had hidden in my pocket with a magician's swiftness. With all my strength, I flung the money into the air, watching them rain down across the room, and laughed as they scrambled to collect the scattered money. Each time they gathered them, I tossed the money skyward again, and soon we were all breathless with laughter, giddy as birds taking flight. That long-awaited paycheck, arriving after our prolonged plunge into poverty's depths, became our feast day, and an occasion for celebration and delight.

The days passed, and the grueling work continued with the same soul-crushing routine. But I never received such a sum from that factory again, due to reduced working hours. Still, my overall financial situation began improving significantly thanks to my factory job.

Another blessing I gained from that factory was memorizing Surah Al-Mulk—The Sovereignty— during work hours, with the help of a coworker named 'Abu Ibrahim,' a young man from the village of Haris. Had I stayed longer at that factory, I might have memorized more chapters of the Quran through this virtuous companionship.

Five or perhaps six months had passed since I started working at that factory. The job had become a suffocating routine, requiring no mental effort— yet it remained grueling for me. The mechanical nature of the labor and the relentless physical demands drained me hour after hour. Yet, throughout that time, I was never assigned the one task everyone found repulsive—the job the workers considered degrading, unhygienic, and beneath them. They avoided it with every trick and ounce of strength they had. For some reason, the factory manager never burdened me with it. Perhaps out of respect for my qualifications, or maybe in loyalty to the promise he had made to Mr. Hani, who had recommended me when I first joined the factory. That vile task was cleaning the damned paint oven—a job required whenever orders demanded color changes, which often happened multiple times a day. The man who emerged from that oven looked like a blackface clown 'Al-Aragoz' or something even more grotesque, splattered with paint while sweeping the oven's interior surfaces with his broom. Every worker took turns in this torment— except me. That changed on my last day at the factory, when the manager, Mahmoud Al-Ghazawi, told me:

"Your countrymen, Khalil, are demanding I make you share in cleaning the furnace like them."
"I don't object," I replied. "I'm at your command whenever you wish."

But fate intervened. That very day, a phone call delivered my salvation. Within days, I escaped that cursed factory forever—spared from stepping foot again in that hellish place.

My Ordeal with Our Kind Neighbor

My relationship with the aluminum factory in the industrial area of Burgan, built on the lands of the neighboring village Haris near my own Kifl Haris, was drawing to a close after that fateful phone call I received while at work—a call that brought deliverance. I will return to reveal the details of that conversation: who was on the other end of the line, what changes it set in motion, and to what shores its currents would ultimately carry me.

But first, let me tell you my story—my ordeal with that legendary man, whose life, qualities, and passions I came to know intimately in his later years, when fate led me to become his neighbor. Our homes were separated only by a ten-centimeter-thick concrete wall, his house standing just beside the house I rented, my uncle's old home. We often crossed paths in the same narrow alleyway—the sole passage I used to reach my dwelling—especially during his comings and goings to and from the mosque.

It is worth noting that my experience with him was a harsh ordeal—lighthearted in appearance, yet a torment in its sting. That day left me circling my own thoughts for hours of anguish before the knot was finally untied, the darkness lifted, and things return to the normal. All of this passed without him ever knowing what had happened, or the depth of the pain I endured on that black day.

That man was the late neighbor Ahmed Al-Zaid—Abu Mithqal—whom I had known only superficially as a child. Our encounters had been breif: glimpses at the mosque or in the alleyway during his brief military leaves, for he served then as a regular soldier in the Jordanian army. Tales of him had reached me—a wise, educated man with a passion for history, heritage, and public affairs—but my knowledge of him remained shallow, fragmented, like shards of light slipping through a sieve. It was only years later, when I returned to Kifl Haris after long exile and happened to take up residence in my uncle Ahmed Al-Asaad's house, right beside his, that I truly came to know him.

Given our proximity as neighbors, and the suffocating emptiness I was enduring during that period, I sought solace in his company. Knowing him to be a seasoned man of wisdom—a polymath retired yet brimming with culture and life experience—I visited his home on multiple occasions. My aim was to know him intimately, to draw from the well of his insight, to learn from the tapestry of his lived adventures, and to exchange stories about his rich, eventful life. And he, in turn, welcomed these visits with open arms. His spirit remained youthful, ever eager to engage with the younger generation. A broad smile often graced his face, even though he was leaning toward isolation.

There was no doubt he endured a harsh childhood, followed by an even harsher military life. Yet his existence was undeniably rich—a tapestry woven with danger, adventure, and hard-won experience. I later learned his father had pulled him out of school early, despite his academic promise, drilling into him the old adage: "Swing the hoe and dig the earth if you want to survive." In those unforgiving times, backbreaking labor in the fields was the only guarantee of sustenance. Tragedy struck young when he lost his brother in a workplace accident— a quarry collapsing on him without warning. Later, he enlisted as a regular soldier in the Jordanian Army, serving on the front lines during the 1967 catastrophe. But military life didn't hold him long. He resigned, returning to Palestine through family reunification, where he spent his remaining years as a farmer—tilling the soil, tending the olive groves he owned.

One evening, he told me about his military service—painting a grim portrait of the wretched life endured by soldiers stationed along the 1948 borders. He had been one of them. On another night, he described the crushing loneliness and gnawing fear that consumed him while guarding those frontlines. There, huddled in fortified trenches at advanced border posts, he would recite protective prayers like armor against danger, incantations to ward off harm. I memorized his prayer verbatim, and have often turned to it as a spiritual armor whenever I sensed peril. The incantation goes:

"Walls, walls, walls—the Throne Verse encircles us, spinning like light wrapped in the Prophet's city. No wind can shake them, no key can break them, till dawn lifts its veil."

I learned that he was an insatiable reader— whose appetite for books had cultivated vast knowledge. Among his passions was documenting the village's history—he kept a weathered notebook filled with meticulous accounts of every significant event. He even kept a sketch of an ancient stone, its inscriptions copied in precise detail—a relic stolen from its place at the Shrine of Prophet Yusha' during the war of '67, vanishing without a trace from the heart of our town.

Among his traditional hobbies—ones he mastered with astonishing skill and flair—was weaving baskets from tender, pliable olive branches. This craft even earned him a modest income. Remarkably, some of the baskets he made remain sturdy to this day, though he passed away, may God rest his soul, in the year 2000.

During one of my visits, we sat sipping tea in the courtyard beneath a lemon tree when he shared with me his lifelong passion: the search for the miraculous wheat seeds mentioned in the Quran— the kind said to yield seven-hundredfold. His voice grew reverent as he quoted the verse: "The parable of those who spend their wealth in the way of God is that of a grain that sprouts seven ears, each bearing a hundred grains."

During one of my visits to him, we sat sipping tea in the courtyard beside the lemon tree. He told me how, throughout his life, he had been deeply devoted to searching for the wheat seeds mentioned in the Qur'an—seeds believed to hold the key to resolving food scarcity. For just as the sacred verse describes, a single grain yields seven ears, and each ear bears a hundred grains: "The parable of those who spend their wealth in the way of Allah, is that of a grain (of corn); it grows seven ears, and each ear has a hundred grains." (Surah Al-Baqarah 2:261).

He told me he was convinced such seeds existed—they were mentioned in the Quran, after all—and so he searched tirelessly until he found them in Irbid. He explained how he'd kept a handful of those rare wheat spikes, hoping to cultivate them and multiply their yield, so people might return to growing that ancient strain. I never learned what became of those golden stalks. By then, the departed was battling fluid in his lungs, yet he endured with quiet resolve, refusing medication, surrendering only to patience as the illness tightened its grip.

I remember that during that time, by sheer chance, our townsman Dr. Yusuf Obeid was present. He worked at the Islamic Hospital in Jordan and treated him for a serious, life-threatening illness—fluid buildup in the lungs. He oversaw his care until he made a full recovery.

During one of our later visits, our conversation turned to antiquities and ancient coins—one of his many passions. He mentioned owning a few artifacts and bringing out two badly deteriorated pieces, their surfaces so worn that any inscriptions or engravings were nearly invisible. He asked if I could research their potential value for him. Carefully, I wrapped the fragments in a paper handkerchief and tucked them into the breast pocket of my white shirt, next to my ID wallet. I guarded them with the weight of a sacred trust—even if they turned out to be worthless.

But alas, as I left our lodgings that morning while my wife performed her daily rituals of cleaning and laundry, she spotted the folded tissue paper peeking from my shirt pocket. Assuming it had been used, she plucked it out without noticing its precious contents and tossed it into the waste bin. Later that day, she threw the bag containing the tissue onto the dump site—that cursed plot of land belonging to Ahmed al-Othman—Abu Tareq, near Al-Rama Al-Shami behind the cemetery. This was where our neighborhood residents discarded their trash, destined for eventual burning in the absence of municipal services.

That day when I returned home, my eyes fell upon the spot where the shirt had hung—dangling from a nail on the wall—but it was no longer there. A surge of panic tightened my chest. "Woman, where is the shirt?" My voice cracked, raw with urgency. "And the paper handkerchief that was in the ID pocket— where is it?" She told me she had thrown them away into the trash.

My mouth went dry as I asked her, "And where is the pouch now?"

She replied that she had thrown it in the rubbish heap, as usual.

I stood frozen, trembling at her words, struck by the sudden realization that I may have betrayed a sacred trust—those rare antique coins belonging to our kind neighbor, Abu Mithqal. A trust so heavy that the heavens, the earth, and the mountains once refused to bear it, as revealed in the Quran:

"Indeed, we offered the Trust to the heavens and the earth and the mountains, and they declined to bear it and feared it; but man [undertook to] bear it. Indeed, he was unjust and ignorant." (Surah Al-Ahzab 33:72).

A crushing weight of grief fell upon me. I struck my forehead in despair, clapped my hands together in anguish, and let out a muffled cry—Oh, what calamity!—as if mountains of sorrow had settled upon my shoulders.

Soon after, my wife and I went to the garbage dump to search for the ancient coins. Firstly, because these artifacts had been entrusted to me as a sacred deposit, and secondly, out of fear that our kind neighbor might suspect I had deliberately hidden them with intent to steal, given their considerable value.

The Devil seized his opportunity and began whispering to me: "You've lost your chance. Even if you become a millionaire someday, your neighbor Abu Mithqal will always believe you owe your fortune to those damned coins."

We quickened our pace, hoping to reach the dump before the coins were buried under mounds of trash—or worse, before someone set fire to the waste piles. Using sticks, we sifted through soiled tissues piece by piece, our eyes darting nervously toward any passersby who might see us and draw the wrong conclusions. In village life, such inexplicable behavior was nothing short of scandalous.

But in our frantic search, we found nothing. I convinced my wife to stop looking and told her, "I will find a way to tell Abu Mithqal about the lost artifacts. If I must, I will swear to him in the Quran so he will believe me."

We returned to our quarters, defeated. Though I struggled to stifle my emotions, my wife saw right through me—the anguish etched across my forehead like storm clouds. Soon, she resolved to return alone to that wretched dumping ground, hellbent to recover what we had lost. I waited for her on pins and needles, praying I wouldn't have to confess our loss to the neighbor.

The minutes crawled by like hours. Perhaps half an hour or more passed when suddenly my wife returned, her face radiant with laughter and joy. She'd found the missing pieces, and her beaming countenance instantly erased the gloom that had darkened my face.

We thanked God for His boundless grace, and my heart swelled with immense joy. Without delay, I rushed to return the coins to their owner. The moment I did, I felt as if two mountains, each as massive as Mount Uhud, had been lifted from my shoulders.

Breaking Free from the
Aluminum Factory's Hell

Here I am, taking you back to the aluminum factory in the Burgan industrial area to tell you the rest of the story behind that phone call - and all that followed.

That factory might have been paradise for the workers who found their livelihood within its walls—men who grew accustomed, over time, to its torments, drudgery, and backbreaking labor, too exhausted to seek alternatives. But for me, it remained an unbearable, suffocating hell. Within those walls, my dreams, ambitions, diplomas, and years of experience in white-collar mental work were buried alive. Worse still were the grueling physical tasks forced upon me—a cruel contrast to the comfortable desk jobs my body had grown accustomed to over a professional lifetime.

As for the positives of working at the factory, it was like a drowning man clutching at straws—a lifeline that came after six months of unemployment and lost income.

Though the three thousand shekels I earned at the end of my first month at the factory never came again - as work hours dwindled sharply with the declining demand for their products - those monthly wages lifted my family and me from the brink of destitution. Payday became our feast day, a celebration as joyous as parched earth rejoicing in long-awaited rain.

The days passed harshly, painfully, slowly, and exhaustingly—made even more unbearable by the absence of any horizon, by the vanishing hope of escaping the torment of that factory in the foreseeable future. I conditioned myself to endure this suffering for as long as fate decreed, unaware of what was being woven for me in the unseen. At the time, my greatest ambition was to transfer to the nearby salad factory, believing its work was far less grueling than the aluminum plant's, and that the wages were better—or so the rumors among the workers claimed.

The truth is, the foreman's demand that I clean the paint oven—just like the other workers—was what finally pushed me to leave the factory. It was the filthiest, most hazardous task in the whole place, brutal on the lungs, and one I had been spared since starting there, thanks to the contractor's recommendation that had earned me some favor. But five months in, under the weight of the workers' insistence—who seemed to resent me for that comfortable exception, had clearly stirred him up. Their demand piled another burden onto my shoulders, deepening my crisis and fueling my disgust for the soul-crushing work in that place. In the end, it only made my decision to leave easier.

In that suffocating darkness, with horizons shuttered and hope all but extinguished—when despair had tightened its noose around my neck and pain coiled about me like a hangman's rope—an unexpected phone call shattered the silence. It came during my shift at the factory, a sudden interruption that would later prove to be my deliverance, a crack of light splitting open the hell I'd been trapped in. On the other end of the line was a man who introduced himself as Mr. Ibrahim Abdul Hadi, the manager of Arabia Insurance Company, headquartered in Nablus within Al-Qasr Hotel building, which the company also owned. Mr. Abdul Hadi informed me that he had reviewed my resume and was interested in hiring me for the company. The offer instantly lifted my spirits, flooding my heart with joy and rekindling my hope of escaping that horrific ordeal. Yet he was quick to caution me, with absolute clarity, that salaries in the country were not like those in Kuwait—I should not expect, nor dream of, a comparable wage.

I didn't negotiate the salary, nor any other terms. I was careful not to ruin the opportunity—this job offer was my promising escape from the grueling grind of the factory. So, I agreed to work with him without dwelling on the details. He scheduled a meeting for the following day, and true to my word, I went to the Arabia Insurance Company's office, located in Al-Qasr Hotel building in Nablus. There, I met Mr. Ibrahim Abdul Hadi in person—a man regarded as one of the most prominent businessmen of that era. On a personal level, I found him to be a charismatic leader with an undeniable presence. Soon enough, he explained that he needed me to help develop the Public Relations Department, in addition to working in the claims division, the most critical sector in any insurance company. All this for a mere 250 Jordanian dinars—the same salary I had earned at the General Products Company in Jordan, despite the cost of living in the West Bank being significantly higher. It was far less than what I had earned at the aluminum factory and a stark contrast to my wages in Kuwait—where, in my last position at Yusuf Ahmed Al-Ghanim's company, this sum amounted to barely 15 percent of what I once took home.

No doubt, the offer was meager, especially since I would have to pay at least three or four shekels in transportation fares just to get to Nablus and back to Kifl Haris. Yet I accepted the offer immediately. My sole, overwhelming concern was escaping that factory—that graveyard—before I had to endure the torture session of cleaning the furnace, a task I was about to carry out due to the pressures and demands of my fellow villagers, as the factory manager, Mahmoud Al-Ghazawi, had already informed me.

And so, I severed ties with the factory—my own personal hell—and began working at the Arabia Insurance Company in Nablus. There, I joined Ms. Oraib Hijjawi in the Public Relations Department, where Mr. Jamal Khoury assisted her as a part-time employee. His role primarily involved publishing an internal newsletter called The Palace's Message, while I worked in the Claims Department under the management of Mr. Qasem Adam, the department head.

Truth be told, I was met with nothing but respect and appreciation from every tier of the company— from the courier all the way up to the general manager. I often felt like the company's golden boy, granted remarkable freedom to maneuver, act, and work as I saw fit—within broad directives, a clear vision, yet always framed by the fundamental principles and concepts of public relations.

As for the Accident Department, the work was limited to documenting incident reports—a routine task I occasionally participated in when time allowed. That job taught me never to sign any document before reading it thoroughly, scrutinizing its contents, and even consulting a lawyer if my signature carried potential financial or legal consequences. This caution, however, was rarely observed when signing an accident report. Most signed blindly—without true awareness, without detailed review, and without carefully examining the wording of the report drafted by the investigator, the accidents department clerk. The investigator drafting the report relied on the informant's statement but took liberties in phrasing it as he pleased, sometimes including details that did not serve the reporter's interest, nor did they fully reflect what the reporter had intended to convey.

No sooner had I began my tenure than I collaborated with my colleague Oraib Hijjawi to draft a roadmap and outline a detailed action plan for the Public Relations Department. Our foremost objective, the one we kept firmly in sight, was to cultivate a positive image for the company, safeguard it, and dispel accusations of monopoly. Beyond that, we aimed to highlight the company's pioneering role in the local community and help it maintain its market share after the entry of rival firms that slashed prices and offered competitive services—leaving Arabia Insurance Company in an unenviable position.

This will also help us strengthen social bonds among employees, harnessing their potential to enhance the company's image by mobilizing them—armed with the right information—to defend it. This will be achieved through an unconscious, indirect mental reprogramming that highlights the company's achievements and its economic and societal role.

As my understanding of the company, its operations, and its position in the market deepened, I crafted a new verbal slogan for it: " Yesterday, Nablus had two mountains—Ebal and Gerizim. Today, it has Ebal, Gerizim, and the Al-Qasr Hotel." From that point on, I endeavored to align all the department's activities around this slogan and its essence, as it embodied the ultimate goal of public relations: crafting a grand, splendid mental image of the company. Naturally, we marshaled every available media and communication tool to achieve these ends. We also took great care to continue publishing the internal newsletter, ensuring it served as the company's voice—showcasing its achievements and initiatives, particularly in the realms of social responsibility and its pioneering economic role in the local economy.

Against all odds, we achieved extraordinary and dazzling success in the department—despite the security chaos before the new regime took over, and the deep-seated hostility toward our company, which had long dominated the market. Then, with the new authorities in place, rival firms sprang up overnight, slashing prices and shattering the Arab company's monopoly over the insurance sector, forcing us onto the defensive.

I remember vividly those early days of my employment at The Arabia Insurance Company, when I struggled desperately to scrape together even the taxi fare to Nablus. The memory remains etched in my mind—those mornings my wife and I spent scrounging for a shekel here, a shekel there, until we finally managed to gather the three shekels needed for the ride. The last of them, after an exhausting search, turned up at the bottom of a straw hat. That day, despite being so new to the company, I was forced to ask for a salary advance.

Mr. Ibrahim Abdul Hadi referred me to Mr. Maurice Nasrallah, the head of accounting. Had I not secured that advance, I might not have made it back to my village, Kifl Haris. To this day, I consider it the lowest point of my life—the sheer depth of poverty I endured.

With my financial situation remaining at its lowest, I managed over time—through my acquaintance with Mr. Jamal Khoury—to devise an infernal plan to increase my income, which I will recount in due course.

What truly upended everything was my colleague, Ms. Oraib Hijjawi. She didn't just change the game for me—she tore open an entirely new horizon, breaking me free from that relentless cycle of pain and poverty. How it happened... Well, I will later share how that came to pass.

A Hellish Scheme to Boost Wealth

There was no doubt that the Arabia Insurance Company operated under extremely difficult circumstances, amid rampant lawlessness and immense societal pressures—all before the Palestinian Authority's arrival and the establishment of police departments, which later played a fundamental role in handling car accidents. Because of this, before the National Authority took over, the Arabia Insurance Company employed a team of tough young men, akin to special forces, to carry out their fieldwork amid the constant tension and occasional attempts at illicit gain. Among them were Zaher Halawa and Medhat Nadi. And, of course, Yasin Abu Ghaush, a former police officer, played a pivotal role in the accidents department.

It's worth noting that the company provided all types of insurance services, not just vehicle coverage. Among the employees handling other general insurance policies were Fuad Hasan, Mutasim Masoud, Moataz Shakaa, Amjad Jaddou, and many others. As for Sami Al-Nemr, he managed the complex health insurance program at the time. Just a few days ago, my former colleague Sami Al-Nemr contacted me and mentioned that he still keeps a group photo of the Arabia Insurance Company employees from when I worked there—and I managed to get a copy.

The company employed teams of robust young men, ready for confrontation, in its security and protection division to safeguard its assets. Among them was a young man named Mahmoud Jbara. I remember telling him one day—this fellow who had caught my attention with his striking presence and charismatic demeanor—that he had the foxy eyes, the kind fit for intelligence work. I even predicted he would rise to the highest ranks in that agency. And remarkably, after the National Authority took power, Mr. Mahmoud Jbara did indeed join the intelligence service and climbed the professional ladder to the very top—exactly as I had foreseen.

Needless to say, working at the company under such circumstances was undoubtedly challenging. Yet soon after the National Authority took power, the company faced difficulties of another kind—chief among them the end of its exclusive monopoly over the market. New competitors emerged, igniting a ruthless price war that severely impacted Arabia Insurance Company's revenues. The company, unprepared to adapt to these market shifts, struggled to maintain its high service standards—whether in pricing, customer care, or claims compensation policies—even after hiring Brian, a retired British insurance expert, as a consultant. Despite his advice, the company failed to adjust to the new reality. It never adopted actionable strategies or programs that could have preserved its dominance in the insurance sector.

In the Public Relations Department, we worked tirelessly to pick up the pieces, mitigate the fallout from those harsh conditions, and strive to help the company retain a reasonable market share—despite the fierce onslaught of competitors. Of course, another crucial task was defending the company's image in the public eye.

Truth be told, with time, the job soon turned into a routine that demanded little effort. Working hours were shortened due to the security situation, and so—under the weight of financial strain, the constant scarcity of cash in my pockets, and the odd surplus of free time—I began to consider taking on part-time work elsewhere after my insurance shift, all in hopes of improving my income.

I had come to know Mr. Jamal Khoury, who worked part-time providing support services for the insurance company. I later learned that he was also an editor and director at "Nablus Today" newspaper, which was headed and managed by Mr. Zuhair Al-Dibie —Abu Islam.

Armed with this knowledge, I paid a visit to Mr. Zuhair al- Dibie at "Nablus Today," a local newspaper whose office occupied the second floor of the Green Market. I proposed dedicating advertising space in the paper at a discounted rate, with us splitting the revenue evenly—on the unspoken principle of "you scratch my back, I will scratch yours."

And indeed, Mr. Zuhair Al- Dibie agreed to the proposal. He was exceedingly kind in his dealings with me, imposed no conditions, and granted me full autonomy over pricing policies and advertising. I immediately set to work, embarking on daily field rounds to sell advertising space to local businesses and institutions. I offered clients a range of options—some small slots at minimal cost, no more than ten shekels per ad, and others larger, more prominent spaces at higher rates.

Many local institutions took advantage of the advertising opportunity, and I have always deeply appreciated those companies and organizations for purchasing ad space—even if just the bare minimum. While advertising undoubtedly benefited them in terms of promotion and increased sales, half of that revenue was absolutely vital to me. It became a vital lifeline that helped alleviate my financial burdens.

Though twenty-nine years have passed since that hellish scheme, every time I walk past the "Tuffaha Shop" for watches near the Cairo Amman Bank's downtown branch, I make a point to step inside and greet its owner, Shams Al Ddin Tuffaha. He remains unaware, of course, that my greeting is really a silent gratitude for the ten shekels he used to pay for advertisements in the Nablus Newspaper back in those bitter days.

The idea succeeded, to a considerable extent. In one month, the revenue reached nearly two thousand shekels—a sum that somewhat eased my burdens for a time. But by that stage, the newspaper was already breathing its last, its existence threatened by the decline of print journalism and, perhaps, by insufficient funding, given that it was distributed for free. And indeed, that was what happened—just a few months after launching that creative scheme to generate extra income out of nothing.

And yet, despite that exceptional extra effort, my financial situation remained precarious, frayed at the edges. My colleague Oraib Hijjawi, who was privy to the company's pay scale and understood which way the winds blew within it, deeply valued my contributions to preserving the company's image. She must have also pitied me—for my salary, despite the tremendous effort I poured in, effort that made a tangible difference, remained at the lowest rung of the pay ladder. Perhaps she could see the poverty grinding my bones to dust.

Meanwhile, I was drowning in a crucible of misery, deafened by static, oblivious to the world around me. But she spotted a silver of hope—a window I could slip through into a fairer, brighter reality. She pointed it out to me, urging me to seize the opportunity, invoking the old adage that a missed chance is a lifelong regret. Yet I hesitated to act on her vision, paralyzed by the weight of accumulated frustration, which had, over time, settled over my heart and mind like a leaden shroud, leaving me feeling powerless. So she took matters into her own hands. She nocked the arrow of change into the bow of my career—and soon enough, I found myself leaping through that very window of opportunity. Ms. Oraib had glimpsed what I could not—that vast new horizons unfolding before me. And indeed, it did. Here, I confess: had it not been for her kindness, her decisive action, I would have surely let that golden chance slip through my fingers. I might have carried the ache of its loss in my heart for the rest of my days.

Strike While the Iron Is Hot

As the saying goes, every era has its own rulers and its men. No sooner had the National Authority returned in 1995 to take control of its territories than the old order was upended. Companies that had operated before the Authority's arrival found themselves grappling with a new reality. The Authority opened doors for new businessmen to establish firms within its jurisdiction, and the insurance sector was one of those shaken by the change.

Multiple companies were licensed, leaving the Arabia Insurance Company—once the sole dominant player in the local market—in a precarious position. It clung stubbornly to its old pricing policies, the same ones that had governed the market before the newcomers arrived. Its efforts to retain customers fell short, for people are always price-sensitive. And so, bit by bit, the scales tipped in favor of the newcomers.

And so, as days passed, those rival companies managed to break into the market, seizing a significant share of the insurance sector. But as every era has its rulers and its men, it became clear that the star of Arabia Insurance Company was now waning. And it wasn't just the competing firms— new businessmen, too, had begun carving out their own place in the market.

No doubt my colleague, Oraib Hijjawi, was aware of those shifting tides—sensing the looming threat to the Arabia Insurance Company. She was close to the decision-makers, the business leader, and had a relative on the company's board of directors.

For all these reasons—and out of sympathy for my wretched financial state at the time, as well as her conviction that I deserved better than the paltry wages I was earning—she surprised me one day with a proposal. "You must seize this opportunity, Abu Ahmed," she said, "with the establishment of a new public shareholding company in the market— Palestine Telecommunications. You should apply for a position there." Yet I received her suggestion with marked indifference, offering only my hesitation as an excuse: "I have no connections there." But she insisted, "I will be your connection." Then, with quiet assurance, she added, "Though in truth, you need no connection at all.

And truth be told, I was surprised by the existence of that opportunity—no, I was astonished to discover an entire Telecommunications Company in its very founding stages, as if I had never once heard of such an economically, financially, and nationally significant venture before that moment. Despite all the standard establishment procedures, the stock issuance and public subscriptions, and the usual accompanying advertisements and public buzz—given that this was an investment opportunity people had eagerly awaited. Though these processes must have been underway for at least a year by that point, bustling with activity, I had failed to notice this major economic development entirely. Perhaps I had heard whispers of it, but I paid no attention; my wretched financial state had pushed it far beyond the bounds of my concern during that miserable period.

I must have been utterly consumed by the relentless pursuit of survival —too preoccupied—with what was happening around me in that vital economic and financial sector—chasing after my daily bread. On one front, I scoured the markets and alleyways of Nablus, hunting for advertisements for 'Nablus Today'. On another, I combed the hills of Kifl Haris, foraging for wild herbs and fruits, anything to ease the crushing weight of financial burdens.

But the most pressing issue—the one that likely consumed my attention and perhaps became my obsession in 1996—was the founding of, and my involvement in, the municipal council of our village, Kifl Haris. The state of the village shook me to the core. The crumbling infrastructure and the dismal public services —it all struck me with brutal clarity, especially when I compared it to the rapid development surrounding us. I had just returned after a long absence, and the contrast was staggering. The village was in ruins, a catastrophe in the shadow of the astonishing urban expansion that had taken hold of the settlement perched atop Jabal Al-Karak. And what twisted the knife deeper was knowing that parts of that very land had once belonged to the people of our village.

Undoubtedly, a significant part of the deterioration in our village's services—a village whose history, as its ancient ruins suggest, stretches back to time immemorial—stemmed from disputes over the municipal council's membership. Personally, I pushed for a consensus-based council, one whose members would be chosen through collective agreement to prioritize the public good, fostering cooperation for the benefit of all. Back then, I even proposed appointing a technocratic council composed of professional experts—the engineer, the doctor, the teacher, the farmer, the contractor, the entrepreneur and so on. The term 'technocracy' was alien to our local community at the time. So much so that my friend and neighbor, Arif Saleh— a high-ranking official in the national authority, may he live long—later remarked, when talk arose of forming a Palestinian technocratic government, that I had been the first to introduce the concept to our local society, ahead of the political class.

Back in those days, I was indeed appointed to a consensus-based council, and I threw myself entirely into making the experiment a success. I mobilized all my energy, my connections, and my knowledge to improve the village's infrastructure, pushing for developmental projects. Among my top priorities was carving out agricultural roads. I remember spending countless days with my friend, the teacher Naim Bouzia, chasing after bulldozers provided to us by Agricultural Relief—thanks to the efforts of Bakr Hammad, then the head of relief operations. We worked tirelessly to cut through the rocky path, one so rugged even pack animals struggled to traverse it, leading toward Dhahr Al-Iraq. This road, which faced fierce resistance from some landowners in the area, gradually transformed into a beautifully paved street, linking the villages of the region together. It made it easier for farmers to reach their fields by car, multiplied the value of the land many times over, and turned the area into lush orchards. Eventually, it became a destination for visitors who would stroll through its shade on foot.

I recall that during that period, I proposed to the director of the Ministry of Local Government in Salfit—the late, fondly remembered Ameen Qubaa—the formation of a joint services council to serve the villages of the region as one united geographic and demographic entity. I even drafted bylaws for this proposed council, which Mr. Ameen Qubaa embraced, offering me his full support and encouragement. I believe that the joint services councils established later, including those still operating today, were conceptually rooted in the very bylaws I had proposed that year.

Yet the consensus council, which I had joined—after a grueling struggle—lasted only ten short months. At that time, to my dismay, I was insulted, and my late father was cursed within earshot. There I faced personal rejection of my ideas, my proposals, and even attempts to diminish my standing. Worse still, some sought to harm me, to cut off my livelihood. In due course, as events unfold in this narrative, I shall recount all that transpired in this regard.

And this was hardly surprising—for with my reformist ideals, inspired by Western democracies, I was like a dancer in the dark. It was only natural that I would face resistance, that conspiracies would weave around me. History makes it abundantly clear: reformers, even prophets, have always struggled to persuade people of the ideas they carried, even when those ideas were divine messages. So why should it be any wonder that my own revivalist, reformist thoughts met with opposition? To be met with opposition was the rule, not the exception.

For all these reasons, I existed in one world, while the whirl of finance and economics around me occupied another. Thus, I was taken aback when this opportunity arose. When my colleague Oraib Hijjawi proposed the idea, it barely registered in my mind. I hesitated, reluctant to submit an application to the nascent Telecommunications Company. Sensing my resistance, she took matters into her own hands. She went down to the hiring office on the third floor—while I shared the Public Relations Office with her on the fourth—retrieved a copy of my CV from my personnel file, and slipped it into a yellow envelope—one I can still picture perfectly. She addressed it to The Hiring Manager, Palestinian Telecommunications Company and summoned the office courier—Abu Saleem, I think his name was. He was an elderly man, his belly sagging with age. She handed him the envelope and instructed him to deliver it to the telecom company's office on the fourth floor of the Abdul Hadi Building downtown, right after he dropped off the mail at the subsidiary insurance office on the building's first floor.

And surely the courier had delivered the envelope as instructed. Although I had put the whole matter behind me, forgotten it entirely—convinced that the hope of a response would be slim—the days proved me wrong in my estimation. Nearly two months later, I received a phone call from the fledgling Palestinian Telecommunications Company, scheduling a job interview in the near future.

The moment I hung up, I was overcome by a sudden certainty—my winds were about to change, and I must seize them. As the poet says, "Strike While the Iron Is Hot." This was an opportunity for a monumental leap in my career and income, knocking at my door, and I swore I would not let it slip away…

As If It Were Deliverance:
The End of My Journey Through
Misery and Woe

The moment the phone call ended—that blessed harbinger summoning me to interview—a tidal wave of joy crashed through me. Hope consumed me, drenching me from scalp to heel in its golden light, as my long ordeal of wretchedness and despair neared its end.

Though the man ever inclines toward stillness, clinging to his safe haven, and loathes change, fighting it tooth and nail with every weapon, conscious or unspoken, even when change bears the promise of deliverance—I nevertheless felt a flutter of hope at this chance that came knocking at my door by some unseen hand. I prayed it would not slip away, that it might finally put an end to those years of misery and wretchedness.

How could it be otherwise? I stood at the threshold of joining a company operating in a vital sector - belonging to what global economic classifications rank as the most crucial economic sector, second only to food and drink itself. This, of course, if fortune smiled upon my aspirations, if my intuition proved true, and if what my eyes beheld was indeed the fountain of life rather than a cruel mirage. For poverty and wretchedness are but another kind of barren desert - where a parched soul might glimpse the shimmering illusion of hope amidst the scorching winds of despair.

This exhilarating optimism also stems from the fact that it is a new company, still in its embryonic stage—barely formed, just beginning to take shape, yet to launch its fieldwork. This means an abundance of future opportunities, and most likely, the founding team will claim the lion's share. And who knows? They may even strike it rich, as if blessed with the Midas touch.

At the same time, I reluctantly leave behind a company long past its prime—aging not just in years but in performance, achievements, and its ability to endure amid market competition. The signs suggested it was in crisis, struggling to stay afloat in the face of unfair competition and measures. In truth, it teeters on the brink of drowning in a turbulent sea of upheavals, changes that imposed themselves as a consequence of the political and operational shifts on the ground— namely, the Palestinian Authority's assumption of control over its territories under the Oslo Accords. This transformation, in turn, introduced new realities that the company would find nearly impossible to navigate without a renewed vision, Herculean efforts, bold administrative decisions, costly and staggering sacrifices, and sufficient adaptability to survive.

For all these reasons— and because every ending is a threshold to all that might be—I went to meet the hiring manager at the Palestinian Telecommunications Company, just as scheduled. I was consumed by a visible, overwhelming eagerness and beneath it a burning, buried fear that this golden opportunity might dissolve like smoke between my fingers. For it would be unbearable to lose the bread at the lip of the mouth.

Ironically, the interview was held at the company's headquarters, located in the Abdul Hadi Building near the roundabout in downtown Nablus. This Abdul Hadi, the owner of the building, was none other than the chairman of the board and director of the Arabia Insurance Company—where I was still employed—the very man who had pulled me out from the suffocating depths of the aluminum factory's prison.

I arrived precisely on time. The first person I met was a secretary, whom I later learned was named Suhair Sarhan. She worked in the orbit of the general manager's office. Moments folded into one another, and soon I was sitting across from the hiring manager. The company's main office at the time was nearly empty, with only a scattered few souls inside—so few I could have counted them on my fingers.

It was evident that the hiring manager I met was fully aware of my detailed, meticulously crafted resume. After asking me a few questions—his soft, silver-white hair and piercing blue eyes marking him as a charismatic, authoritative, and stern figure, much like the archetype of a strict schoolmaster — he wasted no time. He cut straight to the point, asking me outright about my salary at the insurance company: "How much were you making?" I suspect he already knew. Still, I answered honestly: "250 Jordanian dinars."

Before I could even finish speaking, he deliberately dotted the i's and crossed the t's. In a loud, declarative voice, as though clarifying some obscure matter and etching his words into the air, he said: "You will be appointed as an 'Administrative Assistant' in the office of the General Manager. If we were to give you three hundred dinars, you would be over the moon with joy—wouldn't you?" Or at least, that's how he phrased it. But whatever his exact words, the meaning was unmistakable.

In that moment, it was as though a deluge of ice-water shocked me into clarity. 'The mountain labors and brings forth a mouse!' I muttered to myself. What was the point of all that fear?! A crushing disappointment washed over me—after all, they say, "Disappointment cuts deeper than loss." His utterly disheartening proposal nearly provoked me, nearly made me lose my composure. Yet I gathered the fraying threads of my dignity, swallowing the gall of sorrow, the ashes of defeat, the sting of bewilderment. "What else did you expect, Khalil

Effendi?" This cheek is no stranger to slaps, this heart no stranger to swallowing the bile of letdowns. Then, under my breath, I whispered: "Patience, patience… steady now, man. Even the longest night births dawn."

The hiring manager barely waited for my reply. I nodded reluctantly in agreement to the offer, perhaps even forcing a smile, pretending contentment with an offer I secretly resented—all for fear the chance might vanish.

Thus concluded the interview. All that remained was to await the general manager's signature on the employment contract, as the HR director had informed me before I departed. I left the headquarters with my mind adrift, mourning stillborn dreams like infants buried in their cradles. Yet despite this inner turmoil, the scales still tipped in favor of joining the new company—provided matters proceeded smoothly and the hiring formalities were completed.

My wait for the company's final decision was brief—two or three days at most—but long enough to wear my nerves raw. Time stretched into celestial eternities, no longer bound by earthly measure. Such is the torment of a preoccupied mind awaiting a verdict of life or death, where a single day unravels like fifty thousand in the reckoning of a carefree soul.

Finally, I received a phone call from the company. I was told that the General Manager wanted to meet me before signing the contract. The next day, I went once more to the Telecommunications Company's headquarters in the Abdul Hadi Building—this time to meet the General Manager himself. I arrived at the scheduled hour and was ushered into his office. That day, the manager was Dr. Mohammad Mustafa, who had been assigned as an international economic expert to oversee the company's establishment and the transfer of telecommunications responsibilities from the relevant Palestinian Authority bodies to the company.

I greeted Dr. Mohammad Mustafa, who motioned for me to sit at the small round table in the middle of his office. Moments later, he joined me, sitting across with an air of humility, holding what I soon realized was the employment contract awaiting his signature. Seizing the opportunity, I began explaining to the man—whose penstroke would launch my new beginning— just how qualified I was to serve as his administrative assistant. I drew from my advanced academic credentials and years of experience, recounting my professional journey as he listened intently, all ears.

"First, Dr. Mustafa, I worked at Burgan Bank in Kuwait, in the documentary credits department. Then I left for the United States—mainly because the salary was too meager—and earned my

Master's from a prestigious university there: San Diego State University. While studying, I hauled books at a bookstore. After returning to Kuwait with my degree, I joined the Information Center at the Ministry of Information. Alongside that job, I worked in reception at SAS Kuwait Hotel. Later, I became a translation officer at Yusuf Ahmed Al-Ghanim's company in Kuwait. Then, after we were expelled from Kuwait, I served as Assistant General Manager for the auto-parts division at the General Products Trading Company in Jordan. After that, I became a different kind of laborer—working at an aluminum factory in the industrial area called 'Burqan,' built on the lands of the neighboring village, Haris, next to my own Kifl Haris. Finally, I took up a role in public relations and insurance at Arabia Insurance Company, where I still work today."

It seemed I had caught his attention—even his admiration—for my academic achievements and my long, varied experience. Without a word, he plucked the pen from his shirt pocket, struck through the printed job title on the contract, Administrative Assistant, and in his own hand, wrote above it, First Administrator. Then he signed the contract without adjusting the salary to match the upgraded title, leaving it fixed at a mere 300 dinars—indefinitely.

And so I became an employee at the Palestinian Telecommunications Company, headquartered in

Nablus, holding the position of First Administrator under the General Manager. My first workday was December 1, 1996.

My employee number was seven—a digit that placed me in the hierarchy just after the General Manager, the HR Director, a computer technician, an engineer, the secretary, and the General Manager's own driver.

The weight of responsibilities was immense—the company was preparing to take over the telecommunications sector from the Ministry of Communications under the Palestinian Authority. And indeed, that is exactly what transpired, with fieldwork commencing in early 1997.

I adapted to the work environment at the Palestinian Telecommunications Company with remarkable ease. Working with Dr. Mohammed Mustafa was exceptionally smooth. Only a few days after assuming my new role in his office, he called me while he was away on a field visit and entrusted me with signing an urgent document on his behalf. This act made me feel the weight of the responsibility he had placed upon my shoulders.

Then, just twenty days into my work at the General Manager's office, an utterly unexpected shock struck…

The Thunderous Surprise
and the Great Challenge

I mentioned that working with Dr. Mohammed Mustafa was remarkably comfortable, despite his stern and serious demeanor—a man who tolerated no frivolity in the workplace. Truthfully, an employee naturally desires a manager whose qualifications, knowledge, and experience surpass their own. And so it was with Dr. Mohammed Mustafa. He held a PhD from American universities, boasted extensive experience with international financial and economic institutions, and undeniably possessed innate leadership qualities and administrative prowess. I believed his choices for the team around him were shrewd, revealing a keen understanding of character. He surrounded himself with exceptional talents, among them Sam Bahour— that remarkable bulldozer of a man, an expert in his field who valued time like gold. If someone spoke to him on the phone, he'd immediately demand brevity; superfluous words were never permitted.

The team, whose numbers grew steadily after my joining and as fieldwork loomed, also included an engineer named Mona Al-Nashif, as well as Samer Al-Najjar—a cornerstone of the Planning Department—and Samer Al-Birawi, the Administrative Manager. Each was a luminary in their domain.

In December 1996, the company recruited several seasoned engineers from Jordan Telecom to leverage their fieldwork expertise. Leading them was Mohammed Ali, who essentially led the Jordanian delegation on temporary work visas and, upon arrival, he immediately assumed the role of Deputy General Manager. Nabil Tamimi took charge of maintenance, Nael Asaad—a telecom engineer well-versed in internet service—Farid Taha (Subscriber Services Manager), Jamal Salama (Regulatory Relations Director), Taysir Salah (Procurement and Supplies Manager), and Rashad Amous (Planning Department Manager).

The entire team worked like a hive of bees—swift, coordinated, and relentless. Everything was nearly ripe and ready for the official handover of the telecommunications sector from the Ministry of Communications. Soon, work would begin on expanding the network, providing phone lines far and wide, all under the strict terms imposed by the licensing agreement signed with the National Authority.

As I was steeling myself and preparing for the field operations phase—naturally under the mentorship and leadership of Dr. Mohammed Mustafa, which was beyond doubt given he was the architect of our agreement with the Palestinian National Authority and intimately knew every clause of the licensing contract—the celebratory atmosphere was suddenly shattered. At that highly sensitive juncture, a mere twenty days after I had joined his office and begun working alongside him, Dr. Mustafa dropped what felt to me—and likely to his inner circle and employees—like a thunderclap of an announcement: he would be relinquishing the helm, resigning as managing director effective the last day of 1996, just before field operations commenced on January 1, 1997. The justification that later reached my ears was that his role had always been purely consultative—that of a privatization expert tasked with corporate establishment and launch, and that by stepping down, he was clearing the path for those better versed in hands-on field management as the company transitioned to operational reality.

The resignation of Dr. Mohammed Mustafa struck me like a shockwave. At that moment, I felt as though he were leaping off the ship during a critical voyage—abandoning his efforts before reaping their rewards. I feared his departure might destabilize the company and jeopardize my own position. Yet, on another level, I deeply admired his courageous decision. It brought to mind the saying, "Cut your coat according to your cloth." Undoubtedly, such a choice demands remarkable courage and self-assurance, reflecting an unconventional awareness and mindset. For most people in our society, as the proverb goes, "People without taste can't discern the quality of different things"—everything is superficially alike.

No doubt, the announcement of Dr. Mohammed Mustafa's resignation sent ripples far and wide. It also fractured the beautiful dream I had nurtured after meeting him—a dream that left me convinced working under his leadership would be both fulfilling and rewarding. Yet, the turbulence soon subsided when the General Manager's responsibilities were transferred to the Deputy, Abu Ali, a man with extensive experience in the telecommunications sector. Hailing from a background closely tied to the local environment— the Jordanian Telecommunications Company—he brought a sense of familiarity and steadiness.

And so, the long-awaited day arrived— both witnessed and bearing witness, the day of the company's field operations launch drew nearer with relentless speed. In those days, it seemed as if the weight of the world had settled on the shoulders of Engineer Abu Ali. The responsibility was immense, and though he buried himself in office work with unwavering devotion, scarcely lifting his head from his desk—reading, writing, obsessing over the minutest of details—it was clear, at least to my eyes, that he lacked some of the essential qualities of leadership expected of a general manager. Perhaps that was why the board of directors had refrained from naming him as the company's official successor to Dr. Mohammad Mustafa,despite his decades of expertise in the telecommunications sector. Instead, they granted him only the title of Deputy General Manager.

The zero hour loomed. As though it was in the end of the last working day of 1996, the company's staff numbered fewer than twenty employees. Yet, miraculously, the very next day, the telecommunications company swelled to three thousand workers or more. Overnight, it absorbed every employee from the Ministry of Telecommunications under the Palestinian National Authority. They were divided into two regions: The West Bank, led by the charismatic Bahjat Al-Khalidi—Abu Nasri—a man born to command, and the Gaza Strip, under the direction of Engineer Khamis Abu Warda.

There was no doubt that the presence of these two individuals was a decisive factor in the company's success. Under their leadership, discipline was maintained with the utmost rigor. Had they been absent, the company might have plunged into endless chaos—rendering the technical crews, regional departments, and all the assets, resources, and personnel transferred to the company under the agreement and license signed with the Palestinian National Authority utterly unmanageable. Yet their presence ensured operations continued smoothly, as if nothing had changed. The only difference was that oversight now fell to the Palestinian Telecommunications Company's management instead of the Ministry of Communications.

The truth is, drawing from my prior experience as Assistant to the General Manager at a consumer goods trading company, I sensed a palpable absence of certain leadership qualities in the Acting General Manager— may he rest in peace. Thus, with calculated finesse and a touch of benign cunning, I sought to fill part of that void I perceived, especially since Engineer Abu Ali was buried in administrative work, though I took care not to provoke his resentment.

I made sure to trace the veins of the company's operational plans, contractual obligations, and outlined objectives during the licensing-agreement phase of its establishment. I resolved to assist with all the strength, expertise, knowledge, and shrewdness at my disposal to meet those mandated goals. Yet I was exceedingly cautious not to become, in my role as the General Manager's office manager, a bottleneck—or an obstacle—for those seeking access to him, lest it disrupt operations. At the same time, I instilled in everyone a certain awe and reverence for the office, which they respected and adhered to—until the day came when I paid the price for it. I faced an ordeal that nearly destroyed me, and I will recount it to you in due course.

The absence of Dr. Mohammad Mustafa during that critical time added another layer of responsibility to my shoulders. But matters did not stop there—the weight of duty thrust upon me grew even heavier. Only eight days after the fieldwork began and Engineer Abu Ali assumed the role of Acting General Manager, he issued an internal memo to regional managers and department heads, introducing me as the General Manager's Office Director. Just like that, without prior notice, Engineer Abu Ali bestowed upon me a third job title in the span of forty days since joining the company: General Manager's Office Director.

But this title remained like a false promise in terms of financial benefit—never even materializing into ink on paper, much like the second title bestowed upon me by Dr. Mohammad Mustafa: First Administrator.

The new designation, which theoretically expanded my responsibilities—after all, an office manager is not the same as a first administrator— left my pockets just as light. My salary clung stubbornly to 300 dinars, even after this so-called "promotion," the same as an Administrative Assistant's pay.

With this third title acquired in such a short span, and due to the forced absence of Engineer Mohammad Ali—delayed in returning from Amman because of postponed visit permits—I often found myself performing, to a large extent, supervisory duties akin to those of a general manager. These included follow-up tasks, all under the limited authority granted to me merely as his office manager. Still, like a shadow dutiful to its master, I made sure to keep him fully informed of all developments.

Engineer Mohammed Ali held that position for six full months—until a new director, vested with full authority, was appointed to lead the company. Those six months thrummed with a frenzy of relentless activity: the company launched hundreds of projects to expand the network, lay new cables, and connect countless new subscribers. The effort demanded herculean labor, and Engineer Abu Ali, in coordination with regional and departmental managers, permitted overtime work when necessary. And in those days, every case was deemed a necessity. The long overtime schedules would pass through my hands, pages whispering of sleepless nights, before finding their way through internal mail to Engineer Mohammed Ali for approval and payroll processing.

And though I worked long overtime hours with him, nearly every day, I was the only one among all those crowds who never received a single penny in overtime pay.

During those days, I had the chance to escape my poverty and prosper. There were temptations— offers to become a partner to one of the contractors working with the company without investing any capital. But I chose poverty and hardship over what I saw as improper conduct.

And so, the era of Engineer Mohammad Abu Ali came to an end, yet my financial situation and salary remained unchanged. Still, I held onto hope that the winds of change would finally bring rain.

A Manager from Another Planet, and More Signs of Relief

The early days of the Palestinian Telecommunications Company were marked by an unusual calm, despite the frenzied activity surrounding the execution of major projects and critical tasks underway at the time. This tranquility was largely due to the quiet, methodical nature of Engineer Abu Ali, who served as acting General Manager. A man who preferred desk work over the spotlight and media attention, strictly operated within his delegated authority as Deputy Director. He would never make any financial or administrative decisions without first consulting Engineer Abu Tamim—the Chairman of the Board, who kept an office in the company and frequently intervened in strategic matters, as though he were the de facto manager.

My relationship with Engineer Abu Tamim, the board chairman, was exceptionally good. I was responsible for forwarding documents to him for signature as per the authorization matrix. Once, he surprised me by insisting that I review every paper that reached him, verifying its validity and approving it before passing it on—even if it came from senior external consultants. I took this as a gesture of respect for my role and a sign of trust in me as General Manager's Office Director.

On another occasion, I requested his approval to purchase an eighty-dollar manual on office management techniques, published in the United States, hoping to broaden my administrative knowledge. He immediately agreed without hesitation.

But this era of calm came to an abrupt end the moment the company's first officially appointed General Manager, Engineer Abu Mohammed, stepped through the door. With him came a roaring wave of change, as if he were a child of the storm wind.

There was something about his youthful charm—his long, silky hair, especially that rebellious lock of hair dangling over his forehead—his vitality, the way he moved and spoke, his booming laughter, and so many other traits of his personality that made him seem as if he were from another planet. He reminded me so much of my former manager in the Credit Department at Burgan Bank in Kuwait, Mr. Mohammed Al-Naji, who was nicknamed 'The Bulldozer.'

It was clear this man arrived with unshakable determination, armed with years of expertise and an encyclopedic grasp of telecommunications. Nothing escapes him. For every crisis, he had a solution; for every dead end, an escape route. Truly, nothing seemed beyond his reach.

This manager was undeniably charismatic, with an overpowering presence—a true leader, armed with immense courage and an uncanny ability to make decisions, motivate his team, follow through, execute tasks, and deliver results. He considered meetings a waste of time and, when absolutely necessary, would cap them at two hours at most.

He was always in a hurry, and when necessary, he launched crash programs to achieve urgent, lofty goals—like the project to deliver services to Jerusalem's underserved areas. The execution of such emergency initiatives, treated as critical cases, bypassed the usual bureaucratic red tape that could stifle progress or cause delays. Often, he approved exceptional measures if he believed they served the company's overarching objectives, bearing the weight of those bold decisions with rare courage.

There was no doubt that his work with the company propelled it—at an unprecedented pace—toward groundbreaking leaps in service coverage, connecting more subscribers than ever before. Cable extension projects were completed with near-miraculous efficiency, enabling the company to fulfill its contractual obligations in record time. I suspect none of this would have been possible without that consummate professional leading the executive team.

And there was no question about his decisiveness and self-assurance. In one instance, he was preparing to issue a directive requiring department heads to submit daily progress reports. As his office manager—and given the strong mutual respect that had grown between us, along with his openness to my counsel—I advised him, cautioning that such a move might face resistance from influential directors. His response was firm: "People will eventually accept any decision and adapt to it." He stood by his directive despite my warning—and, in the end, he was proven right.

Yet, as the saying goes, "Even the moon has its craters," Mr. Director Abu Mohammed could display startling harshness—sudden flashes of severity that clashed with his otherwise amiability. Just days after joining the company, he asked me to hire an office secretary, insisting she master shorthand—a rare skill among secretarial staff, possessed only by a select few with near-photographic memory, capable of deciphering his rapid-fire dictations transcribed in what seemed like coded language.

The important thing was that we had recruited a candidate for the position who fit the specified qualifications. She was interviewed and had already begun working in the office beside me. The company's main offices were still in the Abdul Hadi Building downtown, and this woman was given preference because she was proficient in shorthand—as noted in her CV among other qualifications, such as her experience in secretarial work. The next day, the manager decided to test her on that skill. He called her in to dictate a passage for her to first transcribe in that coded language, then decode into printed text. The moment she entered his office, he stepped out, closed the door behind him, and instructed me not to help her in any way—this was an assessment, after all.

Only a few minutes passed before she emerged, clutching a sheet of paper covered in scribbles that made no sense whatsoever. She immediately began translating them into English at breakneck speed, typing them up on the computer. As soon as the printer finished, she asked me to review and correct the text—unaware that he had warned me not to assist her. I did glance at it, and despite his orders, I would have helped if I could. But to my shock, I couldn't piece together a single coherent sentence. There weren't even recognizable English words, despite the computer's red squiggles flagging errors. All I could do was reassure her because, no matter what I did, I couldn't decipher the text's subject. When the test period ended, I brought him the disastrous document. I don't know what happened inside that office, but as they say, "You can tell a book from its cover." Her face—pale, shattered—betrayed a deep shock, as if she had endured the worst moment of her life. And his words were harsh enough to melt stone and iron.

But it didn't end there. From then on, every time he entered or left his office, he shot her looks that burned, pierced, exploded. He hurled words at her—not words, but bullets, shrapnel. Staring at her with a mocking lilt, he sneered, "You know what 'shorthand' is, right?" This torment stretched the length of that day. Maybe she hoped nightfall would make him forget or relent, so she returned to work the next morning—though reluctance and humiliation still marked her face. But the moment he saw her, he resumed his verbal teasing, each word quaking her very being, crushing her dreams, turning her life into unbearable hell. In the end, she vanished with the wind, never to return. She quit outright, and I doubt she ever recovered from that bitter ordeal. He could have simply terminated her employment without subjecting her to such humiliation. This young woman's story is to make her a warning example—one that confirms the truth of the saying: "Honesty is salvation," and "lies have short wings." I say this because what happened to her wasn't due to the pressure of the moment, but something far worse.

To that woman—whose fate I never learned after that bitter ordeal—Engineer Abu Mohammed had been so rough to her. But to me and my family, he was our savior, our redeemer, the angel of life and hope. At the time, my family and I were going through an extremely difficult situation, facing unprecedented pressures.

What happened was this: My uncle, from whom I had rented the apartment in our village of Kifl Haris, suffered a stroke after eating what appeared to be an excessive amount of fresh fava beans in the presence of the silent killer—high blood pressure. When he collapsed unconscious, his wife screamed, believing him dead. I rushed downstairs to find him sprawled on the courtyard floor beside a pile of fresh fava beans they had been cleaning for storage. He was rushed to the National Hospital in critical condition. Though he received treatment, he remained in a coma for a long time—until he had consumed the last morsels and drops of his destined sustenance through the feeding tube—before finally surrendering his soul.

Months later, my uncle's youngest son, still a young man himself, began demanding we vacate the apartment so he could marry. Our financial situation made moving to Nablus impossible, and I refused to relocate elsewhere within the village. So I stalled, ignoring my cousin's demands, unable to believe he would actually marry at such a young age. But he intensified the pressure, turning our lives into unbearable hell. Just when the situation became desperate, relief arrived. The General Manager, Abu Mohammed, asked me to move to Nablus so I wouldn't have to return early to Kifl Haris before sunset, allowing me to stay by his side as he worked late into the night. When I told him I couldn't afford rent, he immediately raised my salary by a hundred dinars to cover it. His request—and the raise that followed—felt like a gift descended from heaven. He had no idea of the pressures we were under, nor that his decision had saved us from an incredibly dire situation.

After an exhausting search for an affordable apartment—beginning in the low-income housing districts east of Nablus—we finally found one near both the company and schools in the west. We rented it immediately. I still remember how we decided to buy a wardrobe for our clothes in the new apartment. We went to Makhraz Qalqilya and bought a secondhand pink wardrobe in such a pitiful state that even the carpenter, Mahdi Hassiba, struggled to assemble it. Every nail he hammered in caused another part to collapse. I could see the pity in his eyes, his gaze nearly whispering with sorrow This noble act wasn't the only kindness General Manager Abu Mohammed showed my family and me. Meeting him and working under him marked the beginning of the end for our years of misery, hardship, and poverty. Out of gratitude, I devoted myself to his service, often forgetting my own family to stay by his side. I wielded his authority in matters of discipline, organization, and overseeing progress in the company—all in pursuit of goals and achievements. Until that crisis struck, a bitter trial that left me stranded in darkness. Just when I desperately needed a hand to pull me out, he raised his as if he had never known me. Yet I survived the ordeal miraculously and returned to work with him as before. But a thorn remained lodged in my heart—one that years could not erase.

My Struggle with Envy – The First Trial

I remember how crushing the workload was after the telecom field company launched in early 1997. I was putting in overtime with Mr. Abu Ali, the acting director-general, yet I still had to travel back to my village every evening and return to Nablus each morning—except on weekends, of course. The commute stretched over twenty kilometers, and in those days, the roads were never free of harsh, even terrifying, surprises. Some of them could send a man to the grave.

My financial situation at the time was still at rock bottom, adding yet another layer of psychological strain. There's nothing worse than poverty—and I, too, say: "If poverty were a man, I would bring him to his knees."

Back then, of course, I was still living in the apartment I had rented from my uncle, Ahmed Al-Assad, after we crossed over from Jordan in hopes of reuniting with family. The modest, rural flat stood on Al-Rama Al-Shami, a plot of land in our village, Kifl Haris. The path to it was paved with tombstones, and it lay just meters away from the main cemetery. Through the western window, my eyes would first see an imposing gravestone in the courtyard of the late Jameel Al-Salem's land. To the north, in the plot belonging to the late grandfather Reda Shaqour, another jutting tomb marker stood amid towering fig trees—a green-skinned variety. Southward, several graves lurked beneath an almond tree at the edge of my uncle Ahmed's garden, alongside what I believe was the family burial plot of Awad Haniyeh household. And from the east, you should easily see that the buildings here were erected between graves—or atop them.

This could only mean one thing, written in bold red letters: we were living in the arms of the dead. Reason enough to turn your days into shuddering unease and your nights into a nightmare demanding spiritual armor. These remnants were a ceaseless memento mori—death, that which man flees, yet as God Almighty decreed: "Say, 'Indeed, the death from which you flee – indeed, it will meet you. Then you will be returned to the Knower of the unseen and the witnessed, and He will inform you about what you used to do.'" (Surah Al-Jumuah 62:8).

What mattered was that the relentless pressure of those circumstances had worn me down to a breaking point. That day, I decided to see the late Dr. Zahi Al-Qamhawi—my father's physician and close friend. After listening to my symptoms, he measured my blood pressure with a state-of-the-art digital monitor, a cutting-edge device at the time. The lower reading was alarmingly high, surpassing ninety, while the upper reading was even worse, climbing above one-thirty-five. The doctor turned to me and prescribed blood pressure medication, declaring me a patient of hypertension—medically classified as "the silent killer." But in my case, as the doctor observed, it was anything but silent. According to the doctor, it had sent coded distress signals to my body, forcing it to scream out warning symptoms: faint spells of dizziness.

Despite the danger of ignoring such a warning from a doctor with might and main in medicine, I dismissed it outright—refusing the medication and turning instead to my one beloved 'sports.' And so I did, never missing my regular exercise or cutting back on constant physical activity, no matter how little time I had. Only the most unavoidable circumstances could stop me. For over twenty years, I stayed this course without swallowing a single pill to treat my hypertension, nor did I often permit my blood pressure to be measured. Deep down, I believed that if you fear the bogeyman, you will inevitably summon him into existence.

Yet the sources of stress and upheaval didn't end there. A shake-up in upper management brought in a new director-general—a man who might as well have descended from another planet. His arrival injected fresh blood into the leadership, but as psychology predicts, the existing team spiraled into temporary chaos. Stability would return only once each member had recalibrated their place within the pecking order—of that microcosm.

And with the arrival of that director—a force of nature who carried himself like the emperor of his own domain, wielding unchecked authority—the workload doubled overnight. There I was, at the epicenter of the storm, closest to the director himself. We burned the candle at both ends, laboring round the clock to meet the mounting demands of work, all in pursuit of the targets etched in the work plans. Falling short of these goals could bring harsh consequences—outcomes the company could ill afford.

During that time, I remained active and engaged in efforts to develop our village, Kifl Haris, striving to spark an architectural revival. I spared no effort to attract projects to the village—reaching out to influential figures, lobbying tirelessly. These efforts bore fruit: after my persistent outreach, one organization agreed to restore the dilapidated guesthouse at the village center, which had, over the years, deteriorated into a dumping ground.

Following its renovation, the building was transformed into a sports club—a role it still serves today. My efforts also secured approvals for agricultural road projects. Yet, my relentless activism seemed to unsettle my peers on the municipal council. At a meeting convened by the late Ameen Qubaa, director of the Ministry of Local Government, in his Salfit office to reorganize the council, I felt like Joseph was surrounded by his ten brothers—the council members—as they conspired against me in silent agreement. Their stance was clear: I was a warbler outside the flock. Their hostility cast a shadow of sorrow over the face of the ministry director, who had always respected me and valued my work.

"But the worst of all was what three of the village's so-called knights—one of them a relative—did one day. As I walked down the third-floor hallway of the telecom company's building, I ran into the administrative manager just as he was stepping out of his office. Without preamble, he informed me he'd just finished a meeting with three knights from our village. Surprised, I assumed they must have come to lobby for a telephone network expansion project. What struck me as odd was that they hadn't reached out to me for that purpose. But then, as the manager explained to me at that moment, it became clear that they had come to file a complaint against me. The accusation? A farce so absurd it was tragic—that I was exploiting my position, my job, and my connections with the country's power brokers and wealthy investors' to secure projects for the village. That's what he said—God is my witness.

The truth is, that act left me utterly shattered. Never could I have imagined things would escalate to such a point—that people would repay my goodwill efforts toward the village by trying to cut off my livelihood. They demanded the company restrain me, as the aforementioned manager revealed. Even though he refused to comply. Yet despite my devastation, I buried what I had heard in the deepest well, partly to preserve the peace, and partly so the flames of guilt might keep burning in the hearts of those three knights who had sought to harm me. And from then on, whenever I crossed paths with one of them, hats off to him as if nothing had happened.

After that bitter incident—and with tensions mounting—the municipal council was dissolved. I hadn't stayed long before a three-member committee was formed within the company: myself, Engineer Sami Al-Qaddumi, and the late accountant Yasser Tuqan. The goal was to leverage my position in the company, close to the capital investors, to execute projects supporting educational institutions. We named it the "Support Committee" and opened a bank account at a local bank. To ensure transparency, we stipulated that any withdrawal from its funds required the joint signatures of two members.

For this noble purpose, I led a fundraising campaign—most of which came from the telecommunications company's board members. Once the committee secured a substantial and satisfactory budget, we partnered with Save the Children, then managed by an engineer named Yasser Dweikat, to execute an ambitious project addressing overcrowding at a local school in Nablus. In coordination with the Engineering Department at the Ministry of Education, overseen by Engineer Samir Abdullah, the committee funded this significant endeavor. The project aimed to add an entire floor of classrooms to the Haseeb Al-Sabbagh School in Al-Makhfeyah, Nablus, with our financial contribution exceeding thirty thousand Jordanian dinars.

The committee also funded another project, Ambition, in collaboration with the Nablus Municipality's Projects Department. The goal was to expand the schoolyard of King Talal School in Rafidia during the tenure of its principal, Abu Kishk. Back then, we managed to remove an entire mountain of dirt that stood adjacent to the school, transforming the yard into a space wider than a horse racetrack. Later, it became a full-fledged sports field, an amphitheater, and a vast plaza—finally relieving the overcrowded students who had been crammed into a tomb-like yard.

Additionally, the committee financed an interior renovation project for Zafer Al-Masri School in the Old City, along with several other initiatives—from installing shade canopies to establishing computer centers. Among the schools that benefited from the committee's efforts in setting up computer labs was Kifl Haris Secondary School for Girls, during the era of its principal from the Al-Qadi family.

Later, a few years afterward, I won a prize of one thousand Jordanian dinars from the Cairo Amman Bank. I donated the entire sum to purchase new computers for the Kifr Haris Secondary School for

Girls. The news reached Mr. Abu Khaled—then the chairman of the company's board—through Mr. Waleed Al-Najjar, and he immediately matched my donation with another thousand dinars to upgrade the school's computer lab.

In a parallel effort, with funding from other contributors, we supported over twenty orphaned families—some for nearly two decades—and I made sure their university education was fully funded.

Yet these bitter experiences I endured, though they caused me deep pain, paled in comparison to the greatest ordeal of all: the venom of envy that festered within the company.

My Struggle with Envy –
The Supreme Trial

They conspired an immense conspiracy, but God delivered me, for He knew their deceit. He delivered me from that village—a place where, at that time, my intentions remained beyond comprehension, where my efforts toward reform and progress were met with blindness. They thought the worst of me, yet God turned their malice away and flung open new horizons before me—horizons I could never have reached by my own strength. Their stratagems could not harm me, for God was with me, my ultimate protector. Truly, He is the excellent protector and the excellent helper—so much so that even if their scheming could shake mountains, it would never shake me.

In truth, their actions did not truly harm me—despite the shock, the grief, the ache of betrayal, and the crushing weight of disappointment. They were merely the acts of envious souls, spiteful hearts, or those blind of my true nature and intentions. For I was shielded, on one hand, by unshakable self-confidence and an unassailable sense of worth, and on the other, by knowledge and understanding. Long ago, through relentless study, I had uncovered the hidden link between loss, tribulations, and life's most jarring trials—orphanhood chief among them—as the forge that shapes genius and creativity. I came to understand divine love manifests through suffering; that adversity is a divine crucible, wielded to craft visionaries, prophets, and the extraordinary. These trials are akin to a sacred academy, reprogramming the mind of the tested, refining it until it is capable of birthing brilliance.

If trials held any true evil, or marked a flaw in those who endure them, God would have spared His prophets—the chosen ones, the finest of creation. Yet it was no accident that God made them bear the heaviest afflictions, then the righteous, then the next best, and so on. The firmer a person stands in faith, principles, and conviction, the fiercer their trials—a truth etched into history's witness.

And His Majesty addressed Prophet Moses, saying: "I produced you for Myself," and elsewhere: "That you would be brought up under my eye." These are signs of divine selection, favor, and love. Yet it is clear that the tools of such fashioning—in the lives of prophets, geniuses, and the great—are none other than trials.

People may misunderstand you, deem you mad if you greet tribulations with the same joy as blessings. But the discerning, the wise who have walked through fire, the students of history and the lives of the great—they know. Within suffering lies elevation, a gift often disguised as ruin.

And truth be told, I told myself that leaving the countryside would free me from the cycle of pain and social maladies that typically plague rural life. I ignored the advice of that author on human behavior—whose words I once translated—when he said: " Wherever you go you will find the same smiling monkey faces "

To his words, I would add: In that jungle, you will also find snakes, scorpions, and foxes.
Perhaps it was this very conviction that later dragged me into a new ordeal—one far heavier and more dangerous than the last. This time, it happened in the city, among elitist circles, far from the countryside.

One day, before my move to Nablus, as I drowned— distractedly—in my work at the company, suffocating under its weight, I did what I always did near day's end, just before sunset. I asked the receptionist to call a taxi to take me to Kifl Haris, since the company cars—which usually handled this routine task—were delayed. It was a standard arrangement, approved by the general manager himself. But the employee refused, stalling under the excuse that he lacked authorization—even after I assured him I would take full responsibility, even covering the fare if the manager rejected the expense. Still, he stood his ground.

Undoubtedly, the accumulation of pressures weighing heavily on me like a millstone—the exhaustion of work, the hardships of travel, financial strain, and the belittlement some showed toward my position as office manager for the director-general—all left me feeling humiliated and furious. I must have lost my usual composure, uttering words I considered perfectly justified in such circumstances, though they might seem crude to others. I said, verbatim: 'God damn this situation,' and likely added more colorful expletives. This was idle talk I would habitually repeat in many situations—with or without reason—phrases that never provoked anyone nor caused harm, merely part of an ingrained cultural reflex. A cursed habit, perhaps, and indeed the best habit is to cultivate no habits at all.

And so, the matter ended there that day. I traveled back to my village, thinking it was all behind me— despite the intensity of what had transpired, the heated arguments and sharp exchanges. Yet two or three days later, it became clear that a group of employees had conspired against me in a secret protest movement. They submitted a formal complaint to management, accusing me, among other things, of insulting the company I swear by God—witness to my words—I am innocent of that accusation as the wolf was of Joseph's blood! Yes, I spoke with emotion, but I never cursed the company. I never cursed anyone. There was no reason for me to do so, and foul language is utterly foreign to my nature. How could I insult the company, when its goodness has fed me? It even provides me with a service reserved for senior employees! It's as if the complainant's hearing betrayed him—mistaking the words in Arabic "something" for "company"—or worse, the situation was twisted with deliberate malice by a few envious colleagues who had caught wind of what happened. Their goal? To harm me, driven by some hidden agenda, by the spite festering in their jealous hearts.

What's strange is that the incident was confined to a single moment, a single situation, with a single employee. But what followed was this: a handful of employees—who hadn't even been present, of course—rushed to sign a complaint against me, one that apparently included harsh accusations. Whether out of sheer envy—God knows best—or simply to follow the herd, I still don't know the exact nature of those allegations to this day. I never bothered to find out; they meant nothing to me, and I refused to let them leave a painful scar on my conscience, one that might warp how I treat others.

This prompted the administration to form an investigative committee, which then summoned me for questioning—a shocking, humiliating, and degrading ordeal. Even after all these years, the wound remains deep, raw, tender, and agonizingly painful. I still do not know how I endured it, how I overcame it at all, or how I kept myself from committing some reckless act against my own being.

Though I defended myself desperately, tried to explain my side, even offered to swear binding oaths, the tide had turned violently against me. Even the testimony of the few witnesses—two or three at most—who had seen what happened with their own eyes, must have been swayed as if they had heard only what the accuser claimed. Their statements, it seemed, condemned me. And so, the investigative committee's final verdict was the termination of my employment—period, end of story. That harrowing ordeal became the cruelest test, the deepest fracture, the lowest fall I have ever endured in my life.

Because I was certain of my innocence—of those exaggerated, false accusations leveled against me— I strove with all my might, calling upon my connections with influential figures, to at least overturn the decision to terminate my services. My anguish and torment at the time stemmed not only from the decision itself, which I found unjust and rash, but also from its devastating impact on my family—both financially and socially.

For days, I remained in a state of utter helplessness, left to simmer in the frying pan of injustice. I felt abandoned by all, as if the world had turned against me overnight—suddenly transformed into a bull in a Spanish arena, surrounded by a multitude of gleaming knives. Until at last, I glimpsed a solitary figure in whom I detected a glimmer of hope. I fastened my resolve to him, begged him to pull me from that deadly ordeal—and he did. For this, I remain eternally grateful, indebted to him for my very life. He stood by me with unwavering sincerity, mending my wounded spirit—may God mend his own heart, and the hearts of his descendants until the end of days. His intervention compelled the council chairman to act, mitigating my expulsion to a final written warning, delivered in solemn official script.

That decision became a sword hanging over my neck, filling me with dread and paralyzing my instincts. On one hand, I felt compelled to remain firm in my dealings—to uphold my managerial role and preserve the dignity of the director's office. Yet I was terrified of displeasing others, of provoking yet another complaint, whether petty or justified, that might finally lead to my humiliating dismissal. So I learned to appease. A sheep among wolves— bleating, always bleating—I groveled to win their favor. The slightest flicker of resentment, particularly from those in lower-ranking roles, would send me scrambling to soothe them—kissing their heads, their hands, whatever it took to smother their anger before it ignited another complaint that would spell my end.

This time, the trial was harsh and brutal—almost fatal—were it not for the safety net God had woven for me: the ability to see adversity as hidden grace. Despite the severity of my circumstances, I summoned superhuman effort to absorb what had happened, swallowing my rage and forgiving my adversaries. I treated everyone as if nothing had occurred, even maintaining cordial ties with those whose faces mirrored Abu Bakr's kindness but whose hearts echoed Abu Lahab's venom. I had no other choice; survival among those around me and fulfilling my duties demanded it.

Was this the last of my tribulations in the seven lean years? What was the moment of overwhelming joy I deemed their end? And did my pain later bear the fruit of creativity?

Breaking Free from the Cycle of Pain

The only direction a falling body can take once it hits rock bottom is the opposite one. And when a man is plunged into painful trials, the inevitable outcome is rising—upward, toward glory, success, and triumph.

That great ordeal, which nearly ended my tenure at the company, shattered my life, and cast me beyond the sun, marked the peak of all the fractures and tribulations I had endured in my years—except, of course, for the loss of my mother when I was two years old. No hardship, no matter how cruel or agonizing, can compare to the torment of orphanhood.

It was no easy thing to comprehend what had transpired—especially with the ever-present sword of threat still drawn, poised to strike again. Yet I bore it all with Job-like patience, digesting the pain through wisdom, silence, and a carefully crafted smile that barely contained the fire raging within. Rather than surrender to melancholy, sorrow or isolation, I lost myself in work. Yet I grew cautious in my dealings with people: a brunt child dreads the fire. I learned to test the waters before diving deep—all without letting a soul see that I lived under the shadow of threat, terrified the catastrophe might strike again. For envy thrives in abundance, while true allies dwindle as your stature rises.

Nothing makes a person feel lonelier than being at the top.

I never told anyone about the final warning I'd received as the outcome of that unjust trial—a verdict that kept the noose perpetually tightened around my neck. Instead, I pretended to have emerged unscathed, as the saying goes, "come out smelling like a rose," lest people perceive me as vulnerable. Any such perception would have made it impossible to maintain my role in that hostile environment—especially holding a pivotal position in the company where I was forced to interact with everyone, saints and devils alike, whether I liked them or not.

Truth be told, I didn't notice any drastic change in how people treated me afterward—except perhaps the occasional gloating glances from resentful schemers. My continued presence in the company, defying all expectations of my spectacular downfall, seemed almost miraculous. It became an unspoken testament to my resilience, an implication that I was untouchable—indispensable—in that toxic cesspool of envy and malice. Of course, this could only mean one thing in their eyes: that powerful allies shielded me, preventing my catastrophic collapse.

As for the General Manager, Abu Mohammad, whom I worked under, he never altered his manner of dealing with me. Our relationship remained strong and amiable—though somewhat tinged with my quiet resentment, for I felt he had abandoned me in that critical moment, when I needed his support more than ever.

And truth be told, he had been generous to me from the very moment he assumed the position of General Manager. Under his tenure, my financial situation began to crawl toward stability. Though he advised me never to accept gifts from anyone, he himself showered me with presents. Every time he traveled to Jordan to renew his residency permit and returned, he would bring me a gift—perhaps a bottle of luxury perfume from a world-renowned brand like Cartier, or an exquisite silk tie. No one had ever treated me with such lavishness except the late Mus'ab Khurma, the fifth of seven directors I worked under during my time at the company. That man was an ocean of generosity—not just toward me, but toward many orphans he supported financially, even after his tragic death. His mother took it upon herself to continue his legacy of charitable endowments, hoping it might illuminate his grave. She remained devoted to that cause until her own passing.

Though Abu Mohammad had asked me to hire a secretary for the office—someone to handle routine tasks like answering calls, receiving guests, typing, and similar duties—he always treated me with the utmost respect as his office manager. He made sure I felt the distinction between my role and the secretary's; I was his trusted confidant for major, strategic responsibilities in the office. These included handling correspondence, coordinating meetings, and recording the minutes of administrative discussions. He even assigned me liaison duties with other departments and report preparation—especially board reports. I became something of an advisor to him; he often valued my opinion on important matters—though, in the end, he remained his own man, making independent decisions. This, however, brought him trouble with the board chairman, who had a tendency to meddle in details that fell squarely within the general manager's authority—a classic case of micromanagement.

Abu Mohammad had relocated the company's main offices from the Abdul Hadi Building downtown to the Saad Al-Din Tower in Rafidia, a move driven by rapid expansion and a surge in staff. At the new headquarters, we hired a secretary for the office— per the manager's request—whom I selected from a pool of candidates for her fluent English and years of administrative experience. She became an invaluable support, easing my workload by handling routine secretarial tasks that demanded little mental effort. I mention her now because, later, she and I shared a curious incident—one I will recount when its narrative moment arrives.

And so, with time, life resumed its near-ordinary course, despite the volcano of grief that roared within my heart. Yet as they say—there must always be cracks in everything, for that is how the light gets in. And so, into those bleak, suffocating shadows, a dazzling light suddenly pierced through, rekindling hope in a heart that had nearly turned to dust from the cruelty of people, the bitterness of experience, and above all, the grinding weight of poverty and destitution.

That was the day I learned my name was listed among those eligible for compensation—reparations for the catastrophe that had befallen us in Kuwait back in 1990. We were instructed to appear on a specified date before the responsible committee at the Jordanian Charity Association, in the Al-Mahata district, where the checks would be distributed.

The news filled me with immense joy—though no treasure of Croesus could ever compensate for what we lost in that calamity, with its deep human and emotional scars. Yet the sum now glimmering on the horizon, which we would receive if rumors held true and all went well, did finally materialize just as whispered. After such interminable waiting, after all the exhaustion endured along the way, it felt impossible to believe. This compensation would at last fracture the unbroken circle of our suffering, catapulting us toward financial stability—a sum exceeding our monthly needs, perhaps even compelling me to open a bank account. For the first time in seven lean years, I might see a balance registered in my name.

As the promised day drew near, I secured a mere three-day leave: one to travel to the East Bank, one to collect the check, and one to return to the West Bank.

And so I traveled, bracing myself for every possible complication—my passport had expired in the early nineties, nearly seven years prior. I'd avoided renewing it, fearing I'd be issued a temporary document and lose my right to a Jordanian passport permanently because of the Green Card granted to me upon returning from the United States. No one had considered then that I'd been employed in Kuwait since 1978. But things went smoothly, and I arrived in Bayader Wadi al-Seer, where my father in law had lived. It was the first time I entered their home without him there; he had passed away in late 1996 after a long battle with illnesses that consumed him following the Kuwaiti catastrophe and its aftermath.

I spent the better part of that day at their house, tracking news about the compensation payments. It became clear that the distribution site was in chaos, overcrowded with claimants. I was advised to arrive at the association's headquarters at the crack of dawn—before the sparrows stirred—to secure my place. And so I did, only to find before me a sea of expectant faces, a human tide that seemed to have slept there waiting, their bodies forming an endless queue that swallowed the horizon.

We waited endlessly until the clerks finally arrived and began distributing the checks around eight in the morning. I inched forward with the crowd, slowly, painstakingly, toward the lifeline laid out on the compensation payout tables—until, at last, around eleven, I reached the clerk. He searched for my check, soon found it, and placed it before me. I stood on the threshold of wealth—wealth, that is, in the relative sense. But just as he was about to hand it to me, he asked for my ID. I gave him my expired passport, and when he saw it was no longer valid, he returned the check to its place and demanded a current identification card.

I had never considered this. It hadn't crossed my mind—not once—because I had been allowed to cross borders with it without issue. Now, I writhed in place like a grain in a frying pan, terrified I would have to return to my family empty-handed, my compensation slipping through my fingers. Where would I get a valid ID? How could I possibly obtain one before the end of the workday, as demanded? What a harrowing ordeal, what terrifying moments! What had happened, I wondered? And did I ever get my hands on that check?

If Fortune Favors, Even a Stick
Will Nest Doves

It was truly a shocking and harrowing moment. I stood there stunned, trembling, bewildered, and utterly lost—I didn't know what to do. I nearly collapsed from the sheer weight of the surprise. Just as the morsel touched my lips, it was snatched away! Or perhaps carried off by a merciless wind, leaving me in the grip of desperate hunger.

I had been on the verge of soaring with joy after enduring those long, tedious hours of waiting— hours that began before dawn's first whisper, before the sparrows' chirping. In such agony, minutes stretch into years, enough to drive one mad were it not for the emotional release that comes naturally among fellow sufferers, all waiting in the same plight.

With every step closer to the teller seated behind the desk, my agitation and tension grew. My joy— tinged with wariness and apprehension—reached its peak when I finally laid eyes on the check, so close I could almost touch it with my fingers:

"Pay to the esteemed Khalil Hamad the sum of..." But joy, like a spark, died as quickly as it flared. Just like that—with cruel simplicity—the transaction froze over a trivial technicality I hadn't accounted for: my ID had expired.

The worst of it? I had no time to fix it, even if I tried. The payment window closed at the end of the workday, and by tomorrow, the funds would be rerouted to another group— and so on, indefinitely. I had no idea what would happen to my check then. A crushing weight of catastrophe bore down on my chest. I spun in circles like a drowning man gasping for air, clutching at straws, unsure how to act. At that moment, I knew I needed nothing short of a miracle. The only thought that crossed my mind was to rush and renew my passport—even if just for 24 hours—so I could claim that check.

What pushed me toward this idea—and no other— was hearing that my brother Mahmoud's brother-in-law worked at the Amman Passports Department. He was from the Al-Shalabi family, and I thought, perhaps salvation lies through him.

I stumbled out of the hall, chasing the wind despite the chaos inside me. I hailed the first taxi I spotted and urged the driver to rush me to the Passports Office as fast as possible. And he did—we flew like a storm unchained.

The moment I arrived at the department, I asked for Al-Shalabi. They directed me to the office, so I went to him, introduced myself, and said:

"I'm the brother of your in-law, Mahmoud Al-Hamad, and I urgently need your help renewing my passport—just for twenty-four hours, no more. It's the only way I can collect my compensation check." His response came curtly:

"You have got no choice but to see the Pasha." Then he jerked his chin toward the Pasha's office.
I didn't hesitate to walk straight into Pasha's office. It was immediately clear that he was a kind man— deeply humane in disposition—and I suspected he had Chechen or Circassian roots. He kept his door wide open for visitors—a deliberate gesture to remove any barrier between himself and those seeking his counsel. Even his secretary, who in such cases usually acts as a gatekeeper barring access to the manager's office—sat far from his door, as though she had been deliberately and purposefully kept away.

I greeted him and spoke with courtesy, anguish, and pleading:

"Sir, I need your help to renew my passport—just for twenty-four hours—so I can collect my compensation check before the workday ends."

Meanwhile, the clock hands spun relentlessly, devouring time in cruel contrast to the sluggish morning hours, when they had dragged themselves forward, heavy with indifference.

He replied:
"And why haven't you renewed your passport?"

I said to him:
"Sir, I hold a green card, which means—as per standard procedure—I must wait two weeks for security approval."

He replied sharply:
"Don't worry about that. Just go prepare your passport renewal application and come back to me quickly."

I left him there and hurried to the clerks' office outside the building. I filled out the passport renewal application properly, then rushed back before he could even blink. I was leaping up the stairs to the second or third floor in bounds. When he saw me, he motioned with his hand and said in a hurried tone:

"Hand me your papers."
He scribbled a note to Intelligence on the fax, then gestured again toward a secretary sitting at the far end of the hall—I think her name was 'Aroub'—and told me:

"Give her the documents."
Indeed, I went to her in haste. It was clear she knew her role by heart—the moment she saw me, she took the papers from my hands and told me to come back in exactly half an hour, not a minute more or less.

This time, I was stunned by the speed of it all. The process moved faster than a streak of lightning—no, faster than a gust of wind let loose. I stayed away for precisely half an hour, as instructed, but when I returned, I dragged my feet, still unable to believe what was happening. The very idea of getting a new passport in under two hours—just so I could make it back to the association's office before closing time to collect the check—had been wiped clean from my mind. I had convinced myself that the age of miracles had passed, vanished without a trace.

The moment the secretary saw me trudging slowly toward her, she yelled:

Where the hell have you been? I have been looking for you for an hour!

She handed me the file and hissed under her breath, "Go thank the Pasha."

Later, I thanked God that she had steered me toward this—something I would never have done on my own. The moment I entered the Pasha's office, he stretched out his hand, urging me forward as if the matter now concerned him more than it did me.

He sealed the note with his signature and returned the papers to me.

"Give me the papers," he said. I handed them over, utterly bewildered— Heavens, how oblivious I was!—with no idea what he intended to do. Then, to my astonishment, he penned in his own handwriting:

URGENT / To the Director of Passports, Nablus: Issue passport immediately without delay. With my regards.

He stamped the note with his signature and returned the papers to me.

I could scarcely believe what was happening—no, I was utterly astounded by how swiftly things were proceeding. My God, it was like magic, or something of the sort. Yet, in a flash, I found myself rushing to the director of the Nablus passport office in the adjacent building. The possibility of finalizing the paperwork before the day's end began to feel real, almost tangible. I didn't pause for breath until I stood in the director's office, where I handed him the documents and pointed out Pasha's signature.

Without hesitation, he gestured for me to take a seat on a waiting chair in the nearby corner, then called over an employee and instructed him to expedite the passport. My wait was brief—no more than ten minutes at most—before the manager handed me the new passport, valid for five years. It was no different from the old one, save for the dates of issuance and expiration.

The clock had just struck one in the afternoon when the new passport finally kissed my palms. I leaped into the street like a gazelle fleeing a hunter, forgetting even to thank my brother-in-law, Al-

Shalabi. Joy thrummed in my veins, a wingless bird desperate for flight—hurrying, desperate to reach the employees before their shift ended. The miracle had truly bloomed. I hailed the first yellow taxi in sight and begged the driver to whisk me to Al-Mahata district, the headquarters of the Benevolence and Charity Association, swift as lightning.

And that was exactly what happened. Within minutes, I arrived at the intended association's office and went straight to the clerk who had demanded a valid ID from me that very morning. He had returned the check to the file after realizing my passport had expired—precisely two and a half hours earlier. I handed him the new passport, but his eyes began to whirl like a man on the verge of fainting. He couldn't believe what he was seeing. It was beyond the realm of possibility—no one could obtain a new passport in less than three hours. Hesitating to release the check, he eyed me with suspicion, as if I might have forged the document, then referred me to the supervising manager standing close behind him.

So I went straight to the manager, who stood behind the cashiers, and told him that the Pasha had issued me a new passport to replace the expired one, but the clerk was skeptical. The supervisor took the new passport, flipped through its pages, then held it high above his head and bellowed at the top of his voice:

"This is a proper passport! It's got all the stamps, all the seals… Sirs, hand this young man his check!"
In mere seconds, I found myself staring at the check now between my fingers. Had it not been for shame, I would have smelled it, kissed it. I returned to the same clerk who handed me the check without a word exchanged—he had clearly heard the supervisor's instructions, clear as day.

I left the place feeling as though the dove had truly nested on the peg at last—as though the world had finally smiled upon me and turned in my favor. The season of adversity had passed, receding into the past, and I could seize the moment, take what I desired and longed for, now that fortune had aligned so perfectly, since the tide had turned so auspiciously.

And so, I thought I would try my luck one last time and embark on a mad gamble—who knows, perhaps another miracle would come my way!

Strike While the Iron is Hot – The Greatest Miracle

The moment I gripped the compensation check in my fingers that noon—staring at it with wide, unblinking eyes, once, twice, three times—I pinched myself sharply to be sure I was awake, not dreaming, conscious, not lost in some fleeting illusion. Then I felt my heart dancing with joy, so wildly it might have flown from my chest. And soon, the fever of that uncontrollable elation began to spread, slow and sweet, through every cell of my body, until I trembled and shivered with the sheer thrill of it—such was the wonder, the beauty of that moment.

True, we had lodged our claim for compensation almost seven years before that day—yet deep down, we never truly believed the day would come when those foreign-administered reparations would actually be paid. But it turned out that miracles had not yet vanished from this world.

And I burned with a wild need to voice my joy, to spill it into the world. For a moment, I nearly raced back to my relatives' home in West Amman—to proclaim the miracle—but then I steeled myself and turned east instead of west. I climbed onto the bus bound for Russeifa, toward the Arab Bank branch where my cousin, Rida Shaqour, worked. The whole ride, my knees trembled with the urge to stand up in the middle of the bus and shout that I had received my compensation to every passenger—but I bit my tongue, afraid of their reaction, terrified they would think me mad. Each time the bus slowed down, crawling through Marka and the Shnillar camp, my right foot jittered against the floor, restless as a driver stomping a phantom gas pedal, begging the wheels to hurry.

No sooner had I arrived at the bank than I headed straight to the office of my cousin, Rida Shaqour, on the second floor. He worked in The credit Department, and with his help, I opened a bank account and deposited the check. And just like that—after seven lean years, years where what goes down never comes up—I now had a bank balance exceeding a thousand dinars, more than enough to cover my monthly expenses.

Once the task was done and I had shared my joy with my cousin, I began to regain my composure. The racing heartbeat, the tension—all of it ebbed away, settling back to its natural rhythm.

I left the bank to visit my maternal aunts, who lived side by side in nearby Awajan—just a stone's throw away, their homes no more than two kilometers from the bank. They, too, were casualties of war, much like myself. There was Aisha, Umm Rida, a victim of the 1967 war. After being forcibly displaced from the West Bank, she endured seven lean years, scraping by on the meager income from selling lupini beans and boiled wheat, until her eldest son, Rida, graduated from college and secured a job at the Arab Bank. Then there was Lamya, Umm Majed, who, like me, was among those shattered by the Kuwait Catastrophe. Her husband had worked as a driver for Kuwait's Interior Ministry, spending his spare time toiling as a transporter of passengers and goods in his Monet—a pickup truck. Their suffering was relentless after their forced exodus from Kuwait amid the throngs of displaced in that fateful year. Not long after, her husband, Abu Majid, succumbed to the ravages of illness. My aunt was further burdened by her son, who sank into a crushing depression, leaving the family in relentless anguish—until one of her sons managed to reach the United States through a harrowing odyssey, a treacherous and perilous journey so dramatic it could have been the plot of a Hollywood film.

Because Auntie was a mother to me, this visit filled me with profound joy, infusing my soul with an overwhelming surge of contentment and tenderness. I was enveloped in bliss, in blessing. Before long, I resolved to return to my relatives' home in Bayader Wadi Al-Seer, determined to set out at dawn the following day for the West Bank—where I would rejoin my post as planned.

On the bus ride home, I sat cloaked in solitude, retracing the flickering reel of my memories, pondering this strange and wondrous world—its hidden workings, its cosmic mysteries. I resolved then to seize the chance before me, to wring from it all it could give. For the world had finally turned its wheel, ending its barren cycle after seven parched years that left my family and I had suffered bitterly. Now the winds blew kindly, the gates of fortune and success stood wide open. To let such an opportunity slip away would be more than a regret but, in this case, a sheer and utter loss.

I recalled Imam Al-Shafi'i's poetic words:

When winds of fortune blow, seize them fast—
For every raging storm is followed by calm at last.
And I imagined that if I clutched the earth now— after that miracle, that day unlike all days—it would melt into gold and pure ore between my fingers. Had I squeezed the rocks, water would have gushed forth.

Yet amid that surge of optimism, those overwhelming currents of exhilaration that swept through me as the bus carried me toward Bayader Wadi Al-Seer, something inexplicable came over me. A sudden premonition, as if a whisper brushed against my ears in lucid, audible words: Yes… You must seize this chance. Try again to reclaim the yellow card—but this time, abandon your old approach. You must try a new path—for identical steps will only lead you back to where you began.

Meanwhile, I had reached my bus stop near "Yasser Al-Abadi's" grocery in Al-Bayader. I stepped off just before the bus continued its descent toward Wadi Al-Seer, passing through the traffic light that had just turned green. I proceeded on foot to my relatives' house, each step cementing my resolve. By the time I arrived, I had made up my mind—I would postpone my journey. My restless imagination conjured up a new, audacious plan for reclaiming the yellow card, a path so reckless it bordered on madness. I kept my decision to myself, relying on secrecy to see my plan through, and waited for the next morning.

On the following morning, I headed to the main Interior Ministry headquarters, near the Housing Bank Complex. At the entrance of the ministry building, I encountered a lone man dressed in civilian attire—a crisp white shirt and gray trousers. I approached him:

"Excuse me, sir. Could you tell me where the Interior Ministry's legal advisor's office is?"

He responded with a blend of courtesy, warmth, politeness, and a touch of surprise—as if mine might have been the first inquiry ever made about the ministry's legal advisor:

"And what do you need from him?"

I replied:

"I have a rightful claim with the ministry. He's the one most likely to grant me justice in this matter, being a man of the law."

The gentleman then introduced himself, a broad smile lighting up his face:

"Come with me—I am the head of the bureau."

Indeed, I accompanied him to his office, located just a few steps to the right of the entrance. I believe his first name was Abdullah, though I can no longer recall his surname with certainty. The friendly man asked me to explain my request, so I handed him my old passports bearing my Kuwaiti residence permits. I told him I had been working in Kuwait since 1978, which should have classified me among those eligible for the yellow card. However, the employee at the bridge issued me a Green Card upon my return from the United States—where I had gone to renew my visit visa before rejoining my work in Kuwait. At the time, I had left Kuwait with a valid residence permit, and when I informed him of my employment history in Kuwait, he said:

"Issuing the Yellow Card falls under the jurisdiction of the General Department of Follow-Up and Inspection."

I approached them several times after that, but no one was willing to listen—or at the very least, to consider my request.

Mr. Abdullah picked up the passports, thumbed through their pages, then caught me off guard with a tender gaze. He asked me to fill out a replacement card request—me, who had feared his invitation to accompany him might crush my madcap plan before it even began.

This was the first time an official had actually responded to my request. I stepped out to the scribes stationed outside the building, filled out the application properly, attached copies of our passports, and returned to the gracious man's office to submit the application. He asked me to check back the following day. As I left the ministry building, I was utterly convinced that this time, my request would finally be granted—after such a miraculous breakthrough, it was unlikely the winds of fortune would shift so abruptly. Surely, they would now follow a cycle of blessing and grace.

I returned to him the next day as scheduled, only for him to inform me that my request had been forwarded to the morning meeting. He asked me to come back the following day, and so I did—only to learn it had been rerouted to the police department. The same happened the day after that, with my paperwork shuffled from one office to another, then another.

On the fourth day, I arrived at the appointed time. The moment he saw me, he smiled, then slowly reached for the top drawer of his desk. "I apologize," he said. "They have denied your request." At the same instant, he pulled out the yellow card from the depths of the drawer and handed it to me, his face lit with a radiant grin.

The sight of that yellow card flooded me with indescribable joy. I could hardly believe it—another miracle, greater than the first, had truly happened in just a matter of days.

I thanked him fervently, my voice trembling, yet I still felt I hadn't thanked him enough. This man had welcomed me with nothing but warmth, hospitality, and acceptance—offering not just his office but his undivided attention. He pursued my request with such dedication, such sincerity, as if it were his own cause. He treated me like an angel sent from heaven—not some earthly creature who walks and eats like any other man.

As I stepped out of the ministry building, an unshakable conviction took hold: this pivotal moment was a divine proclamation that the lean years had ended. The season of plenty had begun. And I resolved to march forward and reap the harvest.

Omens and Portents:
The Dawning of Plenteous Years

My joy was immense when I succeeded in reclaiming my rights—receiving the yellow card and discarding the green one. Though I considered it nothing short of a monumental miracle, even greater than its smaller predecessor, my happiness this time was quieter, less tense, less clamorous than the day I received the compensation check. It was as if my reservoir of joy had been depleted by that first miracle, which arrived in the wake of an excruciating crisis. That miracle had been a signal, a sign that the lean years had ended. With its arrival, more beautiful miracles became not just possible, but inevitable—a mere matter of time.

Still on the tug, as the Arabic proverb goes, and I knew I must seize this opportunity to reap a richer harvest. I had witnessed with my own eyes, through the repetition of the miracle, the lean years had passed, and the season of plenty had begun.

And since the bus was climbing, ever climbing, with favorable winds at my back, I resolved to seize the moment. I went straight from the Ministry of Interior headquarters to the General Passport Department, back to the same director I had visited just days before. The same man who, thanks to the Pasha's personal order, the Director-General of

Passports himself—had placed a new passport in my hands within mere ten minutes.

I hailed a yellow taxi near the roundabout bridge of the Interior Ministry, asking the driver to take me to the Passports Department on Second Roundabout, passing through Third Roundabout. Though I sat in the front seat, I clung to a heavy silence, unwilling to entangle myself in empty chatter which neither nourishes nor avails against me. At that moment, I craved solitude—to ponder the great cosmic secret that had saved me from human treachery, flung open doors of providence and grace, and ultimately—through astonishing, miraculous means—granted my heart's deepest desires.

During the relatively short drive, I found myself absorbed in the buildings flanking the road. To the right, the Housing Bank Complex; to the left, a red-hued apartment block beside the Wadi Saqra bridge, its construction stalled for years. Then, the Intercontinental Hotel on the left, followed by Mais Al-Reem Shawarma Restaurant, where I would always relish their mini sandwiches. Eating there became a ritual—one I repeated every time I passed by. The scent of sizzling fat on the skewers would tease my nostrils. Next came the Third roundabout, right beside the restaurant, then Abdeen Grocery on the right as you head toward the Second Roundabout, with the Four Seasons Hotel adjacent. To the left, the gray facade of the Astra Building, embassies, restaurants, and the Abdul Hamid Shoman Foundation—and so it went...

And truly, I was lost in the tides of existential and spiritual reflection when I realized this: That such repeated deliverance from the schemes of men, from their envy, their ploys, their malice and hypocrisy, that this divine alignment—this miraculous, sometimes staggering, earth-shattering ease in the face of trials—cannot possibly be mere coincidence. No, it must be tied to things we ourselves do as human beings. Among them, in my own lexicon, is patience in adversity—beginning and end. The patience that turns fire into coolness, into peace. There is worship, too—and the marrow of worship is supplication. The greatest of which is: "There is no deity except You; exalted are You. Indeed, I have been the wrongdoer." A prayer that carries the promise of answer. There is righteous action, and the highest of it is mending broken hearts—the act that pulls a man back from the brink of ruin. And there are deeds of kindness, the greatest being to serve the orphan and the widow. Its reward? Flourishing and triumph in this life—and in the next, the companionship of the Noble Prophet.

And these rituals are what save you in the critical moment—what unlock the secrets of things and bend people to your will, regardless of their ranks or whims.

It is a treasure stored for you in the bank of the universe, so that when the world closes in on you—vast as it is—and you are convinced all is lost beyond hope, you emerge miraculously unscathed. A sturdy lifeline extends to you from where you neither expect nor foresee, or God orchestrates a miracle for you—one that would never have taken form were it not for that treasure laid aside for you in the universe's vault.

The taxi finally halted in front of the passport administration. I stepped out, awash in a quiet certainty, knowing I would get what I came for—no matter how impossible, even if it meant seeking honey from the nests of mythical beasts.

I headed straight to the office of the Nablus Passport Director—the very man who had issued me a new passport just five days prior, valid for five years. No sooner had I greeted him than I handed over my passport and that vibrant yellow card, its glaring hue betraying its fresh issuance. With measured politeness, I said, "As you can see, I now have a yellow card." His sharp intuition grasped my unspoken request before I could utter another word. He rose from his seat, took a few steps, and passed the passport to a clerk behind the counter. I watched as he pointed with his index finger, lips moving as if delivering precise instructions.

Within minutes, he handed me back the same passport—the only change was the stamp's shape.

The official had wiped away the rectangular stamp visible on the last page with white ink, and once the ink had dried, he pressed a circular one in its place. And so I reaped the first fruits of the yellow card. Now I could obtain a national ID number, an identity card—and for this very purpose, I headed straight to the Civil Affairs Department across the street. There, I secured a family registry, and the next day, I obtained identity cards for myself and every member of my household. With that, I had completed all the formalities required to replace the green card with the yellow one. I was finally ready—prepared to return to my work in Nablus, though my absence had stretched days longer than planned. A forced leave, one I had never anticipated. I didn't know what had become of my job in my absence, nor what awaited me upon my return.

I have always preferred to set out early—even though travel is a sliver of torment, even under the best of circumstances. After bidding my relatives farewell, I left Bayader Wadi Al-Seer at dawn, just as the sun broke over the eastern horizon. I headed west, crossing the bridge toward Nablus. Yet upon returning to work the next day, I was met with a staggering, sorrowful surprise—one utterly unforeseen. Still, I remained composed, steady in my conviction that this too shall pass, that all would be well in the end. Nothing could touch me now, nothing harms me. How could it, when the lean years had faded at last into the past?

Seven Lean Years

And what was it that lay before me, which I deemed a regression? What had transpired, leaving no room for doubt, to confirm the end of those seven lean years?

The End of the Lean Years' Sorrows, and the Dawn of Plenty

And so I left Amman, laden with joy and gifts—a camel's load of them—for the harvest, praise be to God, had been plentiful. The blessings of my journey had surpassed all expectation, all imagination, when only days before, I had traveled there seeking compensation. I would have been content with the sum I received, especially after the check that had nearly slipped away in a critical moment, almost vanishing back to where it came from—had it not been for unforeseen miracles. Had it not been for them, I would have returned to my family weighed down by disappointment instead of gifts and glad tidings. For at that time, securing compensation had been the pinnacle of hopes, the highest of priorities.

Though to cross bridges, barriers, and gaping uncertainties is but a shard of anguish, it is also a shard of hellfire—if you must pass through them into your great prison, endure their degrading rites and terrors to the last measure. It demands Job's own patience. Even those driven through its corridors like flocks do not count this day among God's ordinary days. And the words that chase you as you wait for mercy between the bars of those crushing passageways—which grind you slowly toward the body's inspection, the completion of formalities—are always the same: "It's been a real grind."

Yet during the journey, I caught myself clutching at things as if to keep from soaring—light as a sparrow drunk on joy, eagerly awaiting my family's embrace with a longing fiercer than burning embers—yearning to share the overwhelming happiness flooding through me, that triumphant feeling of the lean years finally coming to an end.

And despite the futility of procedures and the bitterness of waiting, I slipped safely through the eye of the needle. As usual, I celebrated by buying tickets for the red bus that would take passengers to the rest stop, then treated myself to a cup of cardamom tea laced with sage from the little shop just to the right of the exit. The shop sold everything at outrageous prices, no doubt exploiting the wretched state of travelers emerging from the labyrinth of inspections and brief interrogations at the border—their throats parched and near-dust from the ordeal of travel, their desperate need to wet a mouth gone dry with exhaustion and longing.

By the time I reached the rest stop, I had regained some of my strength, shedding much of the weight from the crossing—its lingering exhaustion and worries. When I arrived at the car depot, I instinctively grabbed a box of chocolates from my travel bag as it was being loaded into the orange transport van. It was one of the gifts I'd bought from the duty-free zone. With an air of ceremony, I began handing them out to the bewildered drivers, though I never revealed the reason for my joy, nor my urge to celebrate. I kept it all tucked away, a private delight.

I deliberately chose the seat beside the driver, eager to take in the sight of palm groves flanking the road—left and right. Nearest to the roadside stood an ancient, towering palm orchard, its branches heavy with red dates, visible even from afar as we raced through the meadows like the wind across the lowest point on earth.

By fortune's turn, the Ford's driver abandoned the Za'tara route—whether due to roadblocks or clashes with checkpoint soldiers, we never knew. Our detour wound through Al-Karama crossing, past Al-Hamra's tense barriers, through Al-Nassariya's dust, until at last we reached Al-Badhan: that jewel of springs and orchards that lives forever in my heart as the most beloved landscape of my youth.

Finally, I arrived in Nablus around two in the afternoon. I seriously considered going to the office but decided to postpone it until the next day, guided by the old wisdom: "Better to face things fresh in the morning than weary by nightfall"—and the proverb "Tomorrow is another day." Instead, I spent the rest of that day spinning a tale for my family—one that might as well have been plucked from One

Thousand and One Nights—a story never told before.

The following day, I went to work early, as usual, and tried to resume my duties just as I always had—after first notifying the director of my return and greeting him. Foremost among those tasks was sorting the mail and preparing it for his review.

But to my surprise, my colleague—the secretary I had recruited myself, whom I had chosen from several candidates to work with us in the general manager's office—had apparently taken advantage of my prolonged absence. What was supposed to be a five-day leave had stretched into eight full days, and in that time, she had staged a quiet coup.

On her own authority, she had decided that I was no longer needed in the office. She would take over my role as office manager in my stead—and she began drawing red lines for me.

The implication was clear: I was being sidelined from my role. And since I still didn't know whether the General Director was aware of her coup-like schemes—or if he even approved of them—I decided to tread carefully. I held my tongue, reined in my reactions for a dozen reasons, and told her I'd stay in my office, "talking to the walls," but that she could ask for my help if needed.

So I sat there, door shut, waiting for the director to clarify the situation. Lost in thought, I found myself spiraling through endless calculations. Then the poet's words came to mind:

"I taught him archery day after day...
Once his arm grew strong, he turned the arrow on me."

And with it, the folk saying surfaced in my memory: "We taught them to beg, they beat us to the doors." Indeed, I thought, a man beware—must always guard against the harm that can come from those who do them kindness. I wondered how that creature could even entertain such thoughts as the ones she had voiced. Perhaps she couldn't distinguish between the duties of a secretary and those of an office manager—though I tried to justify her actions, understanding her eagerness to reclaim the prestige she had lost when she left her former role as office manager for a prominent figure in the country, only to become a mere secretary at the telecommunications company.

Lost in thought, I was jolted by the director's booming voice: "Khalil! Where the hell are you, man?" Since my office was right next to his, separated only by a narrow hallway, I heard him clearly. I rushed to him, heart pounding, bracing myself with my hand on my chest, unsure what to expect. He snapped before I could speak: "Where's the mail? Are you asleep?"

My reply came in a trembling whisper, barely audible, though she must have been eavesdropping on our exchange—I replied, "The colleague made it clear—in no uncertain terms—that there's no place for me here anymore." His voice sharpened to a near-shout:

"What did you just say?

He was on the verge of exploding. In that instant, I knew he wasn't part of the coup. So I pivoted fast: "Nothing, nothing at all. The mail will be on your desk, God willing, in minutes."

I hurried out, snatched the mail from in front of the colleague, prepared it properly, and delivered it to the director. For me, things were slowly falling back into place—but it was clear the turn of events didn't sit well with her. Discomfort simmered beneath her surface: tension, resentment, a bitterness that clouded her expression, her mind elsewhere.

Two or three days later, my colleague made a grave mistake—one that harmed no one but herself. It seemed the devil had whispered in her ear, and what does the devil promise except delusion? She wrote a letter to the manager, giving him an ultimatum: either approve her promotion and raise her salary, along with other demands, or agree to transfer her elsewhere if her requests could not be met. She had convinced herself—no doubt under that cursed devil's sway—that I was no better than her.

The manager summoned me to his office after receiving her letter. He showed it to me and asked for my opinion. I responded with heavy silence, though my face likely betrayed my irritation, disbelief, and disapproval of her audacity. He picked up his pen, muttered something unintelligible, and scribbled a note in the letter's margin that read:

"To the Administrative Manager...

Transfer her wherever she pleases."

He handed me the letter, which I hastily tucked between other papers lest she see it. When I left, I personally delivered it to the Administrative Director, pressing it into his hands with the words: "Sooner rather than later." By the next day, the proverb had come true—"Snitches end up in ditches."

Indeed, she was transferred to another department, and I began the exceptional process of recruiting a new secretary. As the saying goes, "Third time's a charm"—and indeed, the third secretary performed her duties within the defined job description, meeting all expectations without causing problems or ulterior motives. We remained, God willing, cooperative colleagues.

Before long, I was assigned additional responsibilities that positively impacted every aspect of my life—especially professionally and financially. I now wore two hats, one for each role, reaping the rewards of those years of plenty.

This appointment marked a qualitative leap with far-reaching consequences. Meanwhile, the General Manager, Abu Mohammad, didn't stay much longer; he left the company at the end of July 1998. In my opinion, his departure was a major technical and administrative loss for the company.

Years of Plenty
The Day I Was Entrusted to be
the Board Secretary

And so, as miracles repeated themselves—each carrying within it astonishing blessings—the vision was confirmed. A cascade of divine favor poured over me and my family, like the relentless rains of January, affirming that the lean and bitter years had passed, receding into memory. Now, we had entered years of plenty: years of abundance where we would sow, press, and reap bountiful harvests. These fertile years dawned upon us, radiant and deepening, with the hope they would last at least a seven-year cycle—just as their seven gaunt years had before.

Yet this didn't mean life would be some eternal paradise—free of troubles and crises, highs and lows. Such a thing was impossible; humans are woven from threads of malice and every wretched trait that poisons existence—envy and spite chief among them. And crises? They endure as long as life itself.

Among the most defining moments that emerged as I escaped the prison of those barren years and stepped into the era of plenty—bringing its gifts in tow—was my appointment as Secretary of the Board of Directors for the telecommunications company, in addition to my role as Director of the General Manager's Office.

I would never have been entrusted with such a sensitive, high-stakes role—one at the very pinnacle of corporate positions—where I sat with leading economists, business magnates, and investors, let alone succeeded and endured, had I not been meticulous, knowledgeable, and trustworthy; capable of handling missions of extreme delicacy that demanded a rare set of skills, typically reserved for academically trained lawyers who'd passed the bar. Without my prior work as a legal translator, which granted me the instincts of a lawyer despite lacking the formal degree, I could never have navigated this daunting task.

Later, however, I enrolled at An-Najah National University to study law, making significant progress in legal principles through courses such as Introduction to Law, taught by Professor Mohammed Sharqa, Commercial Law under Dweikat, Economics with Youssef Abdul Haq, and International Law led by Odeh Odeh. Yet, I was forced to discontinue the program when the university abolished evening classes due to heightened security restrictions and the outbreak of the uprising during that period.

The significance of this role stems from the critical responsibility carried by the Secretary of the Board of Directors. Though the majority of people—even colleagues and executives—fail to grasp its true importance and value, British law and legislators deem it a corporate safeguard. The law explicitly states that in the event of a company's failure or bankruptcy, the first person held accountable—and possibly imprisoned—is the Secretary.

The chairmanship had passed to Mr. Abu Khaled, a billionaire who needed no introduction. Orphaned young, he was the archetypal self-made man, a relentless striver. He once confided in me that his late father had left him nothing but a bundle of company shares. Yet through the years, he forged a legendary success, joining the ranks of billionaires who command awe—the kind whose wealth, as the saying goes, gains three extra zeros. Though in truth, no one knew his fortune's precise measure.

And so it was that I, as Secretary of the Board—whose chairman he was—found myself in the meeting room, glued to his side, seated beside him and at his right hand. I became his right-hand man in all matters of the Board, while the Director General sat with us at the same table, to the chairman's left.

One of my first tasks as Secretary was to document everything said in the Council meetings, particularly the words of the Chairman himself—whose statements were considered final, the distilled essence of all debates and discussions, most of which would later crystallize into decisions, recommendations, and duties.

In one sense, these sessions were, in a way, an extended, low-intensity training course titled "*How to Become a Millionaire: Abu Khaled Pasha Style.*" They spanned twenty years, with a minimum of seven meetings per year.

I had learned it by heart, absorbing every strand of success woven by this genius—this economic legend, this paragon of financial and administrative prowess. Such mastery is often acquired unconsciously, through osmosis and the subtle coding of neuro-linguistic programming, by emulating a role model whose traits collectively shape a person's character. But my learning went beyond fleeting interactions. I recorded council meetings on cassette tapes, later transitioning to digital, and would listen to them again and again, replaying every word until I could distill their essence with honesty, precision, and professionalism—leaving no stone unturned in my pursuit.

I would often listen again and again, jotting down in an external notebook the offhand directives of the Pasha—his insights on managing business and money, turning profits, resolving crises, and making decisions. These were such skills that had crowned him the undisputed sovereign of commerce and finance.

As for the immediate benefit of making me secretary, my salary doubled overnight, and I began receiving an additional allowance to cover travel expenses whenever the Council held its meetings in Amman, Jordan. The Council often convened in Amman's luxurious five-star hotels, and whenever I traveled to attend those meetings, I lived like royalty in those opulent suites. Among the rituals I practiced in those hotels was one I performed the moment I entered my room: a long, steaming bath that washed away the residue of my wretched past and the grime of weary travels. This ritual included half an hour of soaking in the bathtub, submerged in frothy bubbles that enveloped my body and tickled my soul.

Then comes the turn of grilled fish late at night, after spending time between the steaming hot pools, the icy plunges, the sauna, and the steam room. I ask them to bring me Um Ali—Egyptian puff pastry pudding, drizzled with honey—that delectable dessert no one masters quite like the chefs of luxury hotels.

The following day, once the council session concludes and the minutes were recorded— a task more exhausting than any other in my duties—the President would invite us to a lunch so lavish it seemed stolen from the glittering pages of One Thousand and One Nights. It arrived on gilded platters, brimming with love, joy, and legendary generosity. The finest dishes were served at Burj al-

Hamam, one of the restaurants in Amman's InterContinental Hotel atop Jabal Amman.

Yet until that moment, my salary had fallen short of the ambitions that had initially led me to choose the private sector over academia—lured by the promise of higher earnings compared to university professors' modest pay. But the financial leap proved transformative: I began purchasing gold pieces for my wife, who had sold all her jewelry during our lean years just to keep us alive. The company even assigned me a car, for personal affairs after business hours and on weekends, covering all its expenses.

I had become one of the elite, wearing two hats— one as the General Manager's office director, the other as the Secretary-General's right hand.

I now rubbed shoulders with tycoons and business magnates, learning their tricks for wealth—lessons that opened my eyes to investment, especially in stocks and real estate.

Benedictions of the Nameless Soldier: Builder and Economist

The abrupt departure of the General Manager, telecommunications Engineer Abu Mohammad—a man of vast experience in the field—in mid-1998, under circumstances and for reasons not entirely clear, left a gaping void in the company. His sudden leave preceded the appointment of a successor, jeopardizing workflow continuity and managing leave rotations. This vacuum thrust Engineer Abu Ali back into the spotlight, though this time as Deputy General Manager under the oversight of Mr. Zahi Khoury. Despite Khoury's myriad commitments—including his role as director of Coca-Cola—the board had tasked him with steering the company temporarily until a permanent manager could be found.

This assignment from Mr. Zahi Khoury granted me the opportunity to know him more intimately as director of his office—where before, my knowledge of him had been limited, confined to my position as secretary of the board of directors, where he sat as a member.

As the saying goes, "He who doesn't know you is not informed of you"—and over time, I came to realize that this man was truly an unsung hero, a living legend across multiple fields. He was a strategic thinker, an economist of the highest caliber, and one of the foremost figures in business and finance, serving on the boards of several companies. Moreover, he was a leading investor not just nationally, but globally, with significant real estate ventures in the United States. Though he owned numerous properties along Florida's coasts—and likely elsewhere—he still clung, with every fiber of his being, to his home in the ancient alleyways of Jerusalem, residing there whenever he returned to oversee his ventures in Palestine.

He is patriotic to the core, devoted to grand causes—especially the defense of Palestine—laboring tirelessly behind the scenes, far from the glaring spotlight, to see them realized. His mind knows no rest except in his relentless defense of national principles and interests.

He played a pivotal role in safeguarding national interests—economic ones especially. Often, people would witness seemingly miraculous solutions to the most tangled crises, never knowing that behind these triumphs, steering them toward the nation's benefit, stood this unassuming man. A man who, despite being an economic titan—a leading investor, a man of millions— made you feel no psychological or social barriers when you worked with him.

He was deeply humane—compassionate, principled, and tender-hearted. I often marveled at his boundless patience and quiet resilience. It was this very gentleness of spirit that led him to adopt an orphan from the chaos Sabra and Shatila camps, as I later learned, when that storm of violence swept through in the 1980s.

For me personally, I considered him one of the blessings from the years of plenty—a divine gift. After he was appointed to lead the company, his treatment of me was the epitome of kindness, generosity, and humanity. He respected me, valued my qualifications, and trusted my abilities.

I would knock on his door without hesitation or fear, the formal barriers between us now dissolved, seeking his support in raising donations to fund an association I had founded—an informal, personal initiative to support schools. I named it "Support", established long before the company launched its own Communications Social Responsibility Fund, which allocated two percent of the company's annual net profits to finance solutions for crises, provide financial aid to broad sectors, assist individuals with special needs, and fund numerous projects.

At my request, and with the support of Brother Waleed Al-Najjab, the proposal was presented to the council. On multiple occasions and during several meetings, members were urged to donate their attendance fees—compensation they received for council sessions—toward this noble charitable cause.

Thus, the Support Committee succeeded in launching and funding numerous charitable projects. These included adding an entire floor of classrooms at Haseeb Al-Sabbagh School in Nablus, expanding playgrounds at King Talal School in Nablus, renovating Zafer Al-Masri School in the Old City of Nablus, as well as installing shade structures and establishing computer labs in several other schools.

To ensure financial transparency and engineering oversight, I was joined on the committee by two volunteer colleagues: Engineer Sami Al-Qaddumi from the Buildings Department and the late Yasser Tuqan from the Accounting Department.

The funds raised for these noble philanthropic efforts surpassed one hundred thousand Jordanian dinars—the majority came through the direct support of Mr. Zahi Khoury.

From him, I learned countless lessons—ones that stayed with me. I vividly recall his guidance after I was appointed Secretary of the Board, tasked with drafting meeting minutes. He urged me to avoid flowery language, circular debates, and endless elaboration. Instead, he insisted on focusing solely on impactful decisions, recommendations, and actionable tasks approved by the Board. He suggested structuring each page into several columns. The first would state the topic's title; the second, a concise summary of the subject and the key points of agreement. The third column would outline the resolutions, recommendations, and assigned tasks ratified by the Board. A forth column could be added to specify the responsible party for implementation, and a final one to track progress. This way, the minutes distilled the essence of every mind in the room—sharpening the company's performance and ensuring execution, rather than drowning in minutiae.

Yet the greatest blessing of Mr. Zahi Khoury's tenure—for me, both personally and professionally— during his time as the company's General Director came when he, on his own initiative, sent me to attend a training course in London titled "The Role of the Company Secretary in Corporate Governance." The course, organized by a specialized training firm, cost 1,200 dollars in enrollment fees, plus travel and accommodation expenses.

The trainers were lawyers, and the sessions were held at a hotel on Kingsway Street, where we also stayed during our time in Britain. Through that course, I came to grasp the gravity of a corporate secretary's duties—particularly under British law—and my understanding of the role's responsibilities, expectations, and demands grew profoundly.

During that journey, I lived three days straight out of One Thousand and One Nights. My colleague from the auditing department and I would rush out

to roam London's beautiful streets the moment our
training lectures ended. We left no single corner
unexplored—on foot or aboard the double-decker
bus. What I loved most was wandering along the
Thames, that river poets have whispered to in verse.
We visited nearly every landmark: Trafalgar square,
Big Ben, Westminster Bridge, and Buckingham
Palace, where the Queen herself resides. We
shopped at Harrods on Oxford Street, that iconic
artery of the Fog City, and as I walked London's
pavements, I slipped a few pounds into the hands of
homeless souls bedding down on the cold ground.
Following that visit to London—the city of flowers,
fog, and flowing waters—the British Consulate
began sending me an annual invitation to attend
Queen Elizabeth's birthday celebration as "one of
her friends," as the invitation noted.

On one amusing occasion, during Mr. Zahi
Khoury's tenure as director, an unusual item found
its way onto the board meeting agenda under "Other
Matters"—a secondary point I never expected the
board to discuss—was unexpectedly brought up for
debate. That day, I hadn't brought the supporting
documents related to the item with me. As the
discussion unfolded, Mr. Zahi Khoury leaned
toward me and whispered into my ear, asking about
the papers. I replied:

"I assumed you wouldn't need them."

Without hesitation, he picked up a red pen and wrote the English word "assume" on the blank sheet before him—then deliberately split it into:
ass/u/me

With effortless calm and cool composure, he read it to me:

"Assuming makes an ass out of you and me."

There's no need for literal translation here, but the profound lesson remains: "One should never assume"—for assumptions can plunge you into needless pitfalls.

Thus, Mr. Zahi Khoury's tenure as the company's director marked one of the most beautiful and fruitful periods for me. He brought me joy, enriched me with his expertise, generosity, and professionalism—qualities that harmonized perfectly with those abundant years of boundless blessings. Yet, the true leap in fortune and grace came during the era of the director who succeeded him.

The Hybrid Knight:
A Legacy of Circassia and Jerusalem

That valiant knight was a handsome young man—slender, tall, in his early thirties. Highly educated, he held degrees in accounting, management, and engineering from the United States. A hybrid of heritage: Circassia from his father's side, Jerusalemite from his mother's, and Jordanian by identity and belonging. Yet his soul burned with Palestinian longing—proving the adage, 'He takes after his mother's side.' No force but love could have driven him to endure such travel hardships, accept this humble job despite better alternatives, or brave a land so choked with danger and lawlessness. Only his mother's ancestral soil—the land she had left when she parted from his father—could have compelled him.

Strangely enough, he once confided in me that he had traveled alone to Japan as a mere boy—no older than fourteen. That journey had shaped him, hastening his maturity and gifting him wisdom and foresight. For those who travel see, endure, and learn much; those who observe deeply remember deeply. And as the saying goes, a narrow mind is the fruit of an untraveled life.

This young man—charismatic, brimming with vigor and relentless drive—had joined the company's financial division during Mr. Zahi

Khoury's tenure as General Manager. He was part of a handpicked team of Jordanian experts and consultants recruited during the company's founding era, men who crossed the bridge into the Holy Land on temporary visas. It was no secret that he enjoyed close ties with Abu Khaled Pasha, the council chairman, who treated him like family. Nor was it a mystery that he was being groomed to take the helm as General Manager.

Within months, Mr. Zahi Khoury stepped down, and that steel-willed young man with the boyish face—the late Mus'ab Khurma—was named General Manager. His promotion came swiftly after a brief stint overseeing the commercial and financial divisions, while Engineer Abdul Rahman Omar, a dual Egyptian-Canadian national, took charge of technical operations.

Time proved that appointing him to that pivotal, high-stakes role was the right decision—despite his youth and limited technical expertise in telecommunications engineering. He displayed an uncanny talent for management, discipline, and organization, enforcing unpopular policies like the company-wide smoking ban—even in corporate vehicles—which drew fierce backlash from those chafing under his strict measures.

As it turned out, his appointment came at the perfect moment. The company had just completed the bulk of its technical and engineering projects and now needed someone to steer operations with a financial and commercial mindset—precisely where he excelled. His brilliance in these areas triggered a dramatic surge in revenue and profits.

I will confess, I was profoundly skeptical of his leadership at first. His technical experience paled in comparison to that of his predecessors. But time laid bare the truth that a manager's financial acumen and business instincts are the bedrock of corporate success. A leader who disregards financial data when making decisions is no better than a pilot hurtling through the clouds blindfolded—recklessly navigating without the digital instruments right in front of them.

Despite his young age, he possessed unshakable self-confidence, unthreatened by those older than him. This allowed him to interact with me with effortless ease, deferring to my judgment on nearly every matter. Having acquired considerable knowledge and expertise in all administrative and strategic affairs—the company's operational plans, and every related subject—my role in management grew more pivotal beside him. This was especially true during his forced absences when visit permits were delayed.

Our communication was so seamless that I often answered his questions before he even asked them—or delivered what he needed to his office before he requested it. He deeply appreciated this and decided to reward me for my pivotal role in management, particularly as Secretary of the Board of Directors. For the first time since my appointment, he included me in the "bonus" program. The delightful surprise? He treated me fairly, classifying me—in this regard—as one of the senior employees, and began paying me a generous bonus I'd never dared dream of. This significantly improved my financial situation. But lest you imagine he'd unlocked Aladdin's cave of glittering treasures for me, I remained, despite this improvement and the qualitative leap in my finances, unable to afford a home of my own. Instead, I chose to invest as much as possible in stocks.

But it wasn't just that—he went out of his way to please and honor me, a tacit acknowledgement of my role in supporting him to excel as a manager. He gifted me lavish presents; if he ever accepted a gift from someone else, he'd promptly pass it on to me. I still have some of them tucked away: a luxury Rolex, designer neckties I wear on special occasions, even a delicate glass vial for olive oil.

Thus, that period marked a qualitative leap in my income, revitalizing my family's circumstances. To this day, I regard it as one of the most fruitful chapters of the prosperous years—a time of reaping rewards. The butterfly effect of that era lingered throughout my tenure at the company and beyond, even into retirement, as I continued working with them on a consultancy contract. Though his own role as the company's director was cut short—when he returned to Amman to assume a high-ranking position at Cairo Amman Bank—fate did not grant him much time. He fell, his virtuous blood staining the ground.

During his tenure as the company's director, the general situation was exceedingly dire due to the outbreak of a new uprising, plunging us into a state of rampant insecurity. On one occasion, he faced a direct threat within the company from an armed outsider. Without hesitation, I stood by his side, risking myself to stop the man—whose eyes blazed with fury and who wielded a pistol—from harming him. Following that incident, a personal security guard was assigned to him, accompanying him wherever he went.

He had also entrusted me with a new role: Secretary of the company's Executive Committee. This meant overseeing every detail—from convening meetings and preparing the boardroom to recording minutes and following up on decisions... and so on.

Later, he became convinced that I could serve the company better by taking on its most critical financial role. He offered me the position of heading the Commercial Department—a vacancy at the time—yet I chose to remain by his side as his chief aide, despite the financial allure of the department's leadership. This was especially true for the

Commercial Department, the lifeblood of the company's revenue. I sacrificed what would have been a staggering leap in income compared to my current earnings, believing that my place beside him allowed me to play a pivotal role in the company's success. From that position, I could drive progress toward its overarching goals, commercial objectives included.

As for the second reason—the more decisive one—that made me hesitate to accept that tempting offer, it was my determination to remain with the company for as long as possible. I clung to the old adage: "Slow and steady wins the race." Senior leadership roles, after all, were a crucible for those who occupied them, leaving their holders exposed to the wind's path, vulnerable to replacement or outright dismissal if targets went unmet.

Among that knight's most defining traits was his love for charitable deeds. One of the vows he had solemnly pledged—his hand striking his chest for emphasis—was to cover the tuition expenses for my children's university education. Yet, alas, this promise remained unfulfilled. His premature departure from the company, followed by his unjust martyrdom in the bloody hotel attacks that shook Jordan, stole that possibility. He fell, a lifeless hero, within the halls of the Amman Hyatt. His journey ended in the prime of youth, on the cusp of marriage.

The most astonishing irony—one I remember vividly—was that one day when I urged him to hurry with the mail, his response was that there was no need to rush. For a man dies, yet the folders of incoming and outgoing correspondence remain full. And indeed, he passed away with his mail folders still overflowing, as if he had foreseen his death, as if he sensed his hour drawing near.

Yet he left behind a fragrant legacy, as though he had lived by the principle: 'Work for this world as if you will live forever, and work for the Hereafter as if you will die tomorrow.' The hallmark of his life story was sponsoring orphans and a love for charity—may it benefit him in the life to come.

He was a man who cherished goodness, who had compassion for the poor, and who devoted himself to enduring acts of charity, especially for orphans. I swear this and bear witness, for I was his right hand in managing and carrying out this very mission.

One day, I told him how my niece at An-Najah University had mentioned an orphaned student who didn't even have a blanket to shield her from the winter cold. The moment he heard this, he immediately decided to allocate eighty dinars from his own pocket—monthly, of course—to support her. I took it upon myself to deliver the money to her family. But it didn't stop there. Soon, he began urging me to find more struggling families raising orphans so he could sponsor them, offering financial aid until, at one point, nearly twenty households were under his care.

This special program to support widows, orphans, and families in need continued through me even after his death. His late mother, the Jerusalemite woman from the Al-Muhtadi family, took over sending me the funds until she, too, passed away. Yet the program did not end with her—relatives carried it forward for over twenty years. Countless families benefited, and many of their children graduated from universities, all thanks to those contributions.

His love for charity knew no bounds. He would collect used clothes from his affluent acquaintances, hauling them in heavy suitcases to distribute among the needy in Palestine.

Truth be told, I would have been content with his kindness and esteem alone. Yet he lavished upon me abundant blessings, securing for me a labor for the Hereafter—a righteous deed I pray will weigh in my scales of good deeds. It was work to which I had already pledged myself, for it embodied, in practice, my deepest convictions and academic studies: that orphans are the raw material of greatness.

Make Hay While the Sun Shines

They say, "Practice makes perfect"—so there is no harm in revisiting certain matters and concepts. I do not repeat narratives or ideas without great purpose—to etch it deep into memory, so that people may learn and benefit.

And here I say—and perhaps many of you will agree—history and lived experience bear witness that hardships, crises, and trials are, in truth, nothing but grace upon grace—endless gifts and divine blessings. They are like seeds that grow, strengthen, and rise firmly upon their stalks, until the time comes for man to reap their fruits, to harvest and press them.

Yet, for a man to truly harvest that crop—and not fall prey to psychological afflictions, to drowning in the sorrow and melancholy that inevitably shadows hardship and crisis—he must first, second, and thirdly arm himself with patience. No, not just patience: immense patience, endurance, and the will to rise each time he falls.

He must also recognize and accept that the harshness of trials and the intensity of tribulations necessarily signify greater rewards and an abundant future harvest. Indeed, this direct proportionality can yield extraordinary achievements, especially when those trials reach their most painful and unbearable peaks.

Moreover, man must nurture hopeful trust and positive thinking, never allowing negativity to seep into his heart, overtake him, or paralyze him—no matter how cruel or tragic the events may be.

Above all, a person must never expect life to be easy or their path strewn with roses. On the contrary, they must understand that toil, exhaustion, loss, crises, and shocks are simply the immutable laws of existence—that there is no life without misfortunes, calamities, and trials. One must adopt the creed, "What does not destroy me, makes me stronger," as a way of life. Only then can a person await the harvest, no matter how prolonged the darkness of adversity or how fierce its grip.

And so, it was only natural that my harvest in the years of plenty would be abundant—for the pain of the lean years, and those that came before, had not been slight. Nor did I hesitate to reap the fruits of my labor. As the saying my aunt, Umm Rida, so often repeated goes: "Make hay while the sun shines"

While I had personally reaped the blessings of the plentiful years on a grand scale—until at last, their blessings spilled over onto my family. And now, let me share with you one of those laughter-lit moments we experienced together—when my family and I stood together, harvesting what had befallen us and come to pass.

As for me, my life transformed with my improved financial standing—especially after I was appointed Secretary of the Board of Directors. I went from a life of scarcity, poverty, and living among graves to one of luxury in five-star hotels, as though floating in a perpetual state of joy, contentment, and relaxation.

Whenever I traveled to Amman for board meetings—which happened at least once every two months—I always set aside time for relaxation and leisure, taking full advantage of the fact that many of the hotels and tourist facilities were owned by companies belonging to the Pasha, Abu Khaled—who, as it happened, was also the Chairman of the Board. This meant I received generous discounts on my stays at these hotels, all arranged through the office of the Pasha himself.

Beyond the facilities of the Intercontinental Hotel—which, over time, had become my home away from home due to how often I stayed there, and where I enjoyed preferential rates—the tourist spot I loved visiting most was the Movenpick Resort, built right on the shores of the Dead Sea. I frequented that beautiful place, even in winter. On one occasion, I went with my colleague from PADICO's Amman office, Khaled Jaber, to swim in one of the resort's pools. Though open to the outdoors, the water was heated. That day, after we had stepped out of the warm water and settled by the poolside to enjoy a light meal of hamburgers and crispy french fries, a pair of snow-white doves approached us. I remember how those doves caught our attention— mine and Khaled's—yet now, I cannot recall what it was about them that fascinated us so deeply, leaving their image etched in my memory. Just today, I called my friend Khaled and asked him to remind me of that story. But like me, he only remembered the moment, not the tale that had once stirred our emotions and seized our attention so powerfully.

In later visits, whether alone or with a friend, what captivated me most—aside from swimming in the freshwater pools and the salt-heavy sea, or eating light sandwiches by the pool's edge with my lower half submerged—was walking barefoot over sun-warmed rocks and sands from the pools' area, descending that slope until I reached the brine's fringe. There, I would coat my body in the Dead Sea's black mud, then wade into the water with trepidation, fearing the sting of salt in my eyes if my feet slipped—a frequent occurrence despite the ever-ready lifeguard clutching a bottle of fresh water to rinse burning eyes. Then I would return to smear myself in the dark mud once more, repeating the ritual until the sun nearly vanished behind Palestine's mountains.

During those journeys, I noticed something that struck me—people flocked to this place from every corner of the world solely to partake in those muddy rituals, believed to hold healing powers for skin ailments. And even if their physical healing was uncertain, they undeniably restored the soul, revived the heart, and lifted the spirit.

One day, while preparing for a board meeting, Pasha "Abu Khaled" was speaking to me on the phone when he suggested I bring my wife along this time. Without hesitation, I replied, "Then I shall bring both my wife and daughters—provided this trip is on your account." Immediately, I heard him instruct his office manager in the background to arrange the bookings. She coordinated with me promptly, reserving a three-night stay at the Dead Sea's Movenpick Resort—a sea-facing suite for my wife and me, an adjacent room for my daughters Shurooq and Shatha, and later a separate accommodation for my son Amjad when he joined us. Our rooms were secluded wooden chalets, standing apart from the main hotel building, nestled closer to the whispering waters of the Dead Sea.

To avoid exorbitant food expenses—for meal prices at such luxury hotels were astronomical—we secretly smuggled in some light snacks and drinks—a decidedly unconventional move. We resolved to limit ourselves to one proper meal per day, knowing full well that if we had let our appetites run wild, we'd have needed the budget of a small nation.

Yet in that cabin, we lived a "five-star" existence, delighting in every hotel amenity—both our daytime retreats and nocturnal gatherings. The sea's embrace and swimming claimed the lion's share of our greatest joy. Even the aquarium, with its rainbow-colored fish, became a spectacle we would linger beside, watching them dart about in search of sustenance. But when it came to food and drink, we kept ourselves on a tight leash.

The three days passed like drifting clouds, and when the moment of departure arrived, we dragged ourselves toward the reception with the sluggishness of turtles—heavy-limbed and reluctant, wishing our stay could linger a few days more in those enchanting surroundings that made a man forget his sorrows, even his own name.

When we reached the reception, I pulled out my Visa card from my wallet and handed it to the clerk—ready to cover the living expenses, of course, assuming the Pasha had only taken care of the lodging. But the clerk just flipped the card between his fingers a few times before immediately handing it back to me without deducting a thing. Not even a single dinar. He informed me that the Pasha had covered all the costs. And that's when the bombshell dropped. As we left the hotel, I couldn't help but lament all those fish platters—the delicious food and drinks we'd barely touched, though we'd craved them. Had we known the Pasha would cover every expense, we would have sinned shamelessly with seafood banquets, lying awake all night, our bellies croaking like frogs.

But it was not long before my restless thoughts stilled and my heart found solace, as I recalled the words of Imam Ali, may God be pleased with him: 'Time is two days—a day for you, and a day against you. If it is for you, do not grow arrogant, and when it is against you, be patient.' And so I whispered to myself: By God, how truly blessed I am.

A Punishment in Show,
a Blessing in Secret

With the sudden departure of the late Mus'ab Khurma, the reins of management were handed this time to Director Abu Al-Abd—the most highly qualified administrator among all who had previously held the position, though now under the title of CEO. This shift carried its own implications, leaving the role of General Manager at Paltel vacant, awaiting the right candidate to fill it.

This director, under whom I also served as his "office manager" despite my evolving job title, proved to be the most daring, adventurous to the point of recklessness. He operated on the principle: "Better a bad call than no call at all." Thus nothing daunted him—he made decisions back and forth as effortlessly as drinking water or exchanging greetings.

Since decision-making is the essence of successful leaders and visionaries, his extraordinary boldness enabled him to achieve miraculous, unprecedented accomplishments that turned heads in remarkably short time.

In the blink of an eye, he resolved every lingering dispute with the workers' union—issues that had been tearing through the company, threatening its operations, and nearly paralyzing it. He approved most of the union's demands, perhaps even more than they had asked for, injecting a new spirit of combativeness and loyalty among the employees. He even managed to rally the union to his side in a McCarthyite fashion—a maneuver that must be credited to him, and one that marks a successful leader.

His decisions bore substantial fruit, reflected in the company's marked financial improvement and operational expansion—propelling profits to unprecedented heights, both in quality and quantity. The group achieved numerous milestones—both locally and globally. As its financial standing strengthened, profits surged dramatically, and key indicators now pointed to a robust, fiscally stable entity with strategic reserves far exceeding industry norms. It was then that this exceptional director championed the company's expansion, both at home and abroad.

Locally, he established a conglomerate of companies—some specializing in computing, others in media. This particular venture was born at the stroke of a pen, sparked by the glaring gaps in media services and the urgent need to cover a prominent national event. And so, the necessity arose to launch the communications group, of which he became the CEO.

On a global scale, an international telecommunications company was established based on feasibility studies conducted by renowned international research centers. Thus, "VTEL Global" was founded—a subsidiary comfortably majority-owned by the parent company, securing the telecommunications group a dominant and controlling stake. Though this company, considered the international arm of the local firm Paltel, stumbled in several markets, it ultimately succeeded in at least one, significantly boosting the parent company's profits and multiplying its returns.

This "phenomenon" of a manager then listed the company on the Abu Dhabi stock exchange, marking its first trading outside Palestine. Among other effects, this drove the local share price up to 16 dinars—though it soon crashed back to reasonable, fair-value levels.

Yet the company's performance remained strong enough to attract acquisition interest. Kuwait's Zain company made an offer to take over the company, and the deal nearly materialized before collapsing at the last moment for unclear reasons.

Under his leadership, the company also expanded its assets by purchasing land, which later evolved into a real estate subsidiary. This venture held immense future promise, serving as a strategic reserve for the parent company.

Truthfully, the achievements under this extraordinary director with his exceptional managerial and leadership skills—were so striking, so resounding, that they earned him global recognition. He was named one of the Middle East's top leaders.

My relationship with him was excellent. Though keeping pace with his whirlwind decisions was challenging, our rapport remained strong. He never dismissed my opinions when I proposed an idea or answered his questions.

Financially, I benefited from the incentives he introduced for all employees, and beyond that, from his personal generosity. He was a man who valued loyalty and rewarded it.

The truth is, he never let me down in any request I made, and I benefited financially during his tenure—my salary reached the highest level it ever had since I joined the company. Because of this, for the first time since we left Kuwait, I considered buying an apartment to house my family and spare us the burden of paying 200 dinars in monthly rent. And that's exactly what happened: I bought an apartment, paid for it in full—cash on the spot, as they say—signed the deed, and just like that, my family and I were overjoyed, brimming with happiness and pride at this major achievement, the fulfillment of a dream every person yearns for.

Yet, as I was still basking in the euphoria of buying the apartment, preparing with my family to move in,

I received a faxed letter from the chairman of the board. It announced a new nominee to manage Paltel, operating, of course, under the authority of the CEO. Later, this person contacted me, requesting the organizational structure in my capacity as office manager of the director he would soon replace. I promised to send it, as was my duty under the authority granted to him by the chairman's appointment. I had no choice but to comply. But it seems this new appointment hadn't been approved by the CEO—it had been arranged behind his back while he was on leave. As a result, my cooperation with the incoming manager was seen as an act of defiance, despite its legitimacy under the chairman's directive.

Here, politics interfered with management. The CEO's first action upon returning from leave was issue an order removing me from my position as office manager of the general director, replacing me, and relegating me to the role of board secretary only—which meant my transfer to Ramallah, where the group's headquarters were located.

This decision was unjust—and I say unjust because I had never overstepped my authority, not in any way. I had committed no wrongdoing, acted on no personal whim, but had conducted myself with the utmost professionalism and responsibility, strictly adhering to the chairman's decree. That's why my removal was so painful, so humiliating—it was framed as a punishment, drawing smug, yellowed grins from those who had long seen me as a thorn in their sides. I could feel their claws and fangs sinking into my flesh.

To make matters worse, it was catastrophic timing. I had signed the contract for the apartment in Nablus just three or four days before this unjust decision—and I had already paid the full price in cash.

I was stunned by the brutality of the decision, momentarily plunged into a vortex without beginning or end. I spun around myself like one possessed by demons, my thoughts turning to damage control rather than protest—for who could sway the king's decree once issued? My frantic efforts focused on avoiding banishment from Nablus, as such uprooting would have brought catastrophic consequences for my family and me. A local transfer within the same compound seemed the lesser evil.

In this wretched state, I stormed into the CEO's office, my body trembling from the disciplinary blow. I told him I would not resist striping my title as Office Director, but I pleaded not to be relocated to Ramallah—especially since I had just bought an apartment in Nablus the day before. Reluctantly, he agreed to assign me an office in the compound's auxiliary building, far from the General Manager's headquarters.

Immediately, I moved the Board's files to my new office. From that day on, my role was reduced to overseeing Board meetings—a hollow responsibility that left me adrift during long gaps between sessions. To fill the void, I resolved to translate the core ideas of my Master's thesis, which explored the link between orphanhood and genius, into a book. Before long, those ideas crystallized into a manuscript titled Orphans: The Making of Greatness, meticulously polished by my late mentor, Professor Adnan Al-Samman.

The truth is, stripping me of my position as Director of the General Manager's Office was a painful and humiliating blow—like being forced to drink deadly poison. The decision came as a punitive measure, utterly divorced from the blessings of the plenty of years I am about to recount. But those blessings were never meant to last, for as our noble Prophet wisely warned: "No bounty endures forever." And so, he commanded us to toughen our spirits, to brace ourselves always for such bitter shocks and cruel reversals of fortune.

Yet, in alignment with God's words: "Perhaps you hate a thing and it is good for you" (Surah Al-Baqarah 2:216), every adversity may bear a blessing. Had it not been for that decision, the relentless demands of the Director-General's office—consuming time and energy—would never have allowed me to translate my thoughts on the wellspring of creativity into a book. Thus, what seemed on the surface a punishment was, in truth, a divine gift, a mercy from the heavens. I am convinced that the decision did not even originate from the Director's own mind; rather, he was but a vessel to unlock the floodgates of inspiration within me. The result was a book of profound value, dedicated to orphans—a group exalted in over twenty-three verses of decisive revelation. I consider it the crowning achievement of my life, one whose brilliance and significance I may never surpass, for it addresses matters of utmost importance.

Through the pages of that book, I was able to incorporate the findings of my study on the relationship between orphanhood and genius. The results revealed that 54 percent of the sample—comprising the hundred greatest figures in history, as listed in Michael Hart's book—had lost one or both parents before the age of 21. Thus, I succeeded in providing statistical evidence for the validity of my Positronic Theory, which posited that the link between orphanhood and genius was one of cause and effect.

This theory laid the groundwork for another, offering a hypothetical explanation for the source of creative energy—how adversity sharpens intellectual capacity and, consequently, creativity. This proposition, which still awaits scientific validation, is neither heresy nor sophistry. Rather, it is derived from physics, which speaks of a fifth fundamental energy—beyond electrical, electromagnetic, and cold and hot atomic energy—known as positronic energy.

It is as though God is embedded within the human mind particles of anti-matter and matter, so that when tragedy strikes, these particles collide, generating positronic energy—an inexhaustible wellspring of mental vigor, its intensity directly proportional to the magnitude of suffering.

And so, this achievement came as one of the blessings borne from the trials I endured—beginning with the sting of early orphanhood, and ending with the sting of being stripped from my post as Director of the General Manager's Office. That humiliation was a sharp slap to the face, jolting me from my professional slumber and guiding me, as if by divine inspiration, toward what I consider my greatest triumph.

Days passed, and the CEO transformed into a true legend—an emperor ruling a vast empire, all by the sheer force of his achievements. But time turned its wheel, and by the summer of 2009, his tenure in telecommunications came to an end when he resigned for reasons unknown. His resignation was, regrettably, accepted—proving the old adage right: no one is indispensable. Meanwhile, I remained in my role as Board Secretary, and later, I was assigned an additional position with new responsibilities and extra pay, steadily improving my financial standing.

Remnant Blessings from Years of Plenty, Drifting to Me Bashfully

$\mathcal{S}$ hortly after the telecommunications company launched in early 1997, the Chairman at the time—Abu Tamim—handed me two phone numbers and instructed me to contact their owners, both of whom were working in the United Arab Emirates. I was to inform them that the Chairman awaited their return to join the telecom company. It turned out that both men had previously worked with him at PADICO.

I made the calls as requested. They returned almost simultaneously and soon joined the telecom company's team—one in the Financial Department, Abu Al-Makarim, and the other, Abu Al-Safi, who was appointed to the Auditing Department.

As days passed and Jawwal Company was established, Abu Al-Makarim was transferred to head its Financial Department. Jawwal was a separate entity but wholly owned 100 percent by the telecom company.

My interactions with Abu Al-Makarim remained limited and superficial, even after he rose to become Jawwal's Financial Manager and later its General Manager. This continued until the resignation of CEO Abu Al-Abd, prompting the Board to appoint an internal successor. Their choice fell upon Abu Al-Makarim as the new CEO, effective early 2010.

This choice marked a dramatic end to an era of ambitious—and at times reckless—expansion for the corporate group. The new CEO's cautious temperament stood in stark contrast to his predecessor's adventurous, empire-building persona. His management vision, shaped by a purely financial background, was fundamentally rooted in cost-cutting. Likely, the timing of his arrival—coinciding with firsthand knowledge of the prior expansion's financial fallout—only deepened his resolve to adopt an austerity-driven approach, making slashing expenses a cornerstone of the company's strategy.

This principle remained a defining hallmark of his tenure in the highest executive office—more than the pursuit of launching new projects. It was rooted in the American adage: A penny saved is a penny earned. It is worth recalling that in one of his earliest speeches to a gathering of employees at the dawn of his tenure as CEO, he openly declared his intention to reassess the status quo, stating plainly: "We will build upon what succeeds and dismantle what fails." His determination to divest the subsidiary companies was evident from the outset—he saw them as financial burdens that strayed beyond the core mission of the parent company. This objective remained among his aspirations until, years after assuming his position, he succeeded in divesting two of the five subsidiaries by selling them to their employees—though he had long justified their existence as vital, supportive arms of the company's central operations.

From the outset, with his restrained and unconventional managerial and financial approach—centered primarily on cost-cutting—he sought to shed the burdens of the sprawling technical administration, which had already accomplished the bulk of the technical work but had since become a colossal cost center. Ultimately, he succeeded in establishing independent companies, owned by the very technical employees themselves. The parent company then contracted them to carry out technical work as external outsourcing partners. This move relieved the organization of immense financial strain, improved its fiscal health, and kept profits aligned with successive budget plans— despite conceding a portion of the market share to competitors who had managed to penetrate the industry and establish a foothold that only expanded with time.

Moreover, this initiative granted employees the opportunity to found their own firms, employing large numbers of workers and securing respectable incomes for them, rather than resorting to early retirement or outright termination. It also contributed to maintaining reasonable profitability and stabilizing the company's financial standing.

As part of his broader cost-reduction strategy, he implemented an ambitious and sustained early retirement program, significantly slashing administrative expenses by buying out years of service from numerous employees—many of whom were no longer essential after the network's completion and the shift in operational demands. This voluntary program was executed in phases.

Meanwhile, he succeeded in expanding the network, enhancing its technical infrastructure, and building upon prior achievements, including the company's external service growth. He put an end to all unsuccessful and unviable ventures within VTEL's globally sprawling projects, while salvaging the company's sole branch—which he now managed directly. Over time, it became a lucrative operation, transforming into a profitable and successful enterprise: the parent company's external arm. This turnaround came after years of stagnation during which it had incurred substantial losses.

Under another administrative expense item, a program was implemented to provide employees with car ownership, aiming to reduce the costs of the company-supplied vehicles previously reserved for senior staff. Although the company incurred substantial expenses to fund this project, it gradually freed itself from the heavy financial burden of maintaining company cars.

Undoubtedly, this conservative fiscal policy, along with cost-cutting through well-planned initiatives, not only safeguarded the company's achievements but also strengthened its financial standing and profitability. Under his leadership, financial indicators reached their peak—despite fierce competition and turbulent geopolitical conditions.

Against all odds, he even succeeded in expanding the cellular network—enabling the company to keep pace with global telecom giants. This, despite the relentless obstacles and external pressures besieging the enterprise, challenges that persist to this very day.

My relationship with Abu Al-Makarim remained cordial and perfectly amicable from the moment I first knew him—when I had him brought in to work for the company. Though unlike his predecessors, I never worked directly as his office manager. Our interaction was confined to my role as Secretary of the Board of Directors, despite the paradoxical fact that, administratively, I reported to him in his capacity as CEO. Our bond grew stronger after he assumed the executive presidency, yet it remained restrained, never transcending the bounds of formal dealings.

During his tenure, I personally benefited from the vehicle ownership program, acquiring my own car approximately a year and a half before reaching sixty—the age of retirement. In those days, I lived in constant fear of being excluded from the program due to the payment structure that required employees to settle the car's price through monthly installments extending beyond my remaining service period. Yet he raised no objection. Perhaps he overlooked that particular detail at the time, for had he noticed, he might have taken a different stance more aligned with his conservative nature— that uncompromising disposition which would never sacrifice the company's interests, not even by a hair's breadth.

Perhaps he knew I would remain with the company in the same position after my status was reviewed with the board chairman—the ultimate decision-maker in such matters. And indeed, that's what happened, though under a fixed-term consultancy contract renewed annually. Or perhaps he had foreseen and intended to deduct the remaining installments from my entitlements upon retirement—which also came to pass.

Yet his generosity toward me was not limited to that project, which allowed me to own a car in my name for the first time since we left Kuwait twenty years earlier. He was also remarkably generous in financial matters—I received my full fees, and upon reaching retirement age, an additional token of gratitude: a piece of musk, in recognition of the many roles and duties I had undertaken throughout my years at the company. Each of these positions demanded the utmost knowledge, effort, concentration, dedication, and nerves of steel.

Among them was my assignment as secretary of the executive committee of PADICO—the parent company and majority shareholder of the telecommunications firm. This role also proved financially rewarding, as PADICO paid me a lump sum for each session. I invested these earnings in stocks from the financial market, eventually building a solid portfolio that now yields me substantial annual dividends.

Although large numbers of senior employees like me were granted early retirement during his tenure, I continued working until I reached retirement age—and even beyond, staying on in the same role past sixty. Most likely, this was at the directive of the Chairman of the Board, as I was subsequently relieved from regular attendance after being reappointed under a consultancy contract. From then on, I handled board affairs remotely as needed, no longer bound by office hours, ensuring my presence wouldn't set a precedent other might question.

I can say with certainty that my continued role as Board Secretary under a consulting contract after turning sixty surely bore the Pasha-Chairman's fingerprints. Once, while standing beside him in his Amman office, his office manager asked—within earshot of several attendees, perhaps in jest—why I still held my position despite my age and the many changes in leadership. The Pasha replied: "Because the Undersecretary is more vital than the Minister, and the Town Clerk more essential than the Mayor. He safeguards the institution's continuity and integrity."

Despite my shift to a fixed-salary contract, I remained on the list of those entitled to the year-end "bonus," and I continued to benefit from this substantial bonus for two or three more years. Then, I was removed from that list, and those payments were suspended under the guise of cost-cutting, even though my responsibilities remained unchanged, except for being exempted from regular attendance.

There was no doubt that losing the bonus marked a significant drop in my income—an early omen, a warning that I stood on the precipice of another cycle of lean years. That feeling only deepened, starkly so, when my consulting contract with the company was abruptly terminated at the age of sixty-seven—a cruel coincidence, as it aligned with the outbreak of that wretched pandemic.

Had the vision proven true? Was I truly on the brink of another seven lean years? Would the coming drought consume all I had reaped in the years of plenty?

Back to the Beginning—Had the Lean Years Come Again?

My brother-in-law, Hashem Jaber, resides in Nablus—as did his father before him, who had served as a policeman during the British Mandate in the 1930s and 40s. Over time, the family settled permanently in the city, gradually transitioning into commerce. Hashem Jaber became a true son of the marketplace, and markets are the finest schools indeed. There, one comes to know people intimately—their temperaments, psyches, and behaviors—gleaning wisdom from every encounter and transaction.

Sometime after my return from Kuwait, I found myself consulting him about business matters. It was then he recounted the tale of a merchant from Jenin who had inscribed above his shop entrance: "Beware the Thorns." When Hashem inquired what thorns he meant, the merchant explained this was a warning against three pitfalls no prudent person should ignore: never entangle yourself in partnerships, agencies, or guarantorships.

It was a profound lesson—one I committed to memory and made an article of faith in my personal code. From that moment, I resolved never to involve myself in any of the three, no matter the circumstances. Yet life has a way of cornering a man, of stripping him of his balance in hard times.

It can force him into choices that defy his convictions, his knowledge, even his deepest fears. And so it happened to me—inevitably. After the CEO's decision to remove me from the office of the General Manager, reducing my role in the telecommunications company to that of a mere secretary, I was struck with a devastating blow that shattered my equilibrium. I felt as though my expulsion from the company was now imminent. In the wake of that horrific shock, I relinquished one of that accursed triumvirate and, to my profound regret, entered into a partnership with ten others— colleagues of mine from the same company.

The company had actively encouraged its staff to establish independent telecom service providers, acting as distributors for its own services. At the time, the telecom market was wildly enticing, full of promise—and that allure ultimately dismantled my defenses, paving the way for my plunge into partnership.

And so it was that the eight of us founded a company with a capital of one hundred thousand Jordanian dinars. We, the eight, held 80 percent of the company shares, while the owners of a small pre-existing market firm that we absorbed— received the remaining 20 percent. Each of them owned 10 percent of the new company's shares and also served as employees within it.

The new company launched into operation, but as the saying goes: "Too many cooks spoil the broth." The business soon faced countless hardships, and with each passing day, failure grew more entrenched—exorbitant spending on wretched, futile advertising campaigns, employees whose sole concern was maximum profit with no sense of loyalty, an incompetent management, and a merciless market... And so it went.

In short, the company stumbled almost from the outset. Perhaps it would have been wiser to shut it down early, but greed—the delusion of revival and eventual profit—kept us clinging on. If only we had aborted the venture then! We were chasing a mirage.

Time passed, and then one of the partners demanded to withdraw from the partnership, offering to sell his share—valued at ten thousand dinars when the small company, of which he was a co-owner, had been acquired. He insisted on selling his stake for the full amount, even though the company's collapse had diminished the fair value of its shares to barely ten piasters. None of the other partners agreed to buy his share at the inflated price. Left with no other choice, the partner—in a fit of spite— sent me, as chairman of the board, a formal legal notice through the court, threatening to file a lawsuit against the company laden with malicious, baseless accusations!

The bitter tragedy lies in the fact that in the early days of the company, I had been the one to help bring this person from his distant homeland to work with us—yielding to the pleas and relentless insistence of one of his relatives. The justification was his elderly parents' need for his presence, coupled with his rare specialization. As time passed, the company was on the verge of terminating his employment after the project he was hired for was discontinued. Yet, once again, moved by pity, I intervened, and he was transferred to a position that granted him a better income than before.

Even so, that man repaid every kindness I had ever shown him with utter disregard. He succumbed to the whispers of human and jinn devils alike, and in a moment when darkness had swallowed his heart, he resolved to blackmail me. Knowing the sensitivity of my position in the company—and that I would likely yield to his unjust demands to protect my standing and livelihood—he resorted to a devilish scheme: threatening legal action with baseless accusations, charges that would condemn him as much as anyone, given he was complicit as a partner.

It had never crossed my mind that any of my partners could act in such a shocking manner— especially this person, considering all the help I'd given him that had made him wealthy. He would never have attained what he did without my unequivocal support, to the point where even some of my fellow employees and friends would occasionally criticize me for standing by him.

Yet he did what he did, and in that moment, I felt it was the worst of my life. A call came from the company's reception desk—a clerk summoning me downstairs to receive a legal notice from the court. I complied, still reeling from the shock of it all. Soon, I found myself facing two choices, each more bitter than the last: either I could maneuver to contain the fallout, swallow his blatant blackmail, and shield my career from ruin (a path both possible and plausible)—or I could look him dead in the eye and say:

"Go ahead, knock yourself out," and sacrifice everything I had built.

In the end, I chose appeasement to save my career. I paid him the exact amount he demanded—down to the last penny—even though his contribution wasn't worth a damn at that point. On top of that, I was forced to pay an extra two thousand dinars in legal fees to the lawyer he'd hired to pursue the case. That was where things ended with him—but not with me. By God's will, I will hold him accountable for his injustice before the Almighty—"Before God, all disputes are settled."

This incident undoubtedly set a precedent. Soon after, the owner of the other half of shares in the small company we had acquired also demanded to sell his stake—claiming he need liquidity for a new venture he had launched. Though he never said it outright, his very offer came armed with unspoken inevitability, forcing me to buy his shares under the same rationale, paying no more than half a dollar per share, despite their fair market value hovering near zero at the time.

With time, the company began to operate smoothly after the new partner and board member took over management. It soon ranked first among telecom agency firms for years to come. Yet that success never translated into financial stability—no significant profits were ever recorded. The excuse? The crushing weight of startup debts, which had devoured its capital with startling speed.

Though some friends advised me to dissolve the company and shut it down—seeing no real benefit in keeping it running. But I viewed it as a social institution, a window of charity, at the very least, for its employees who depended on it. Chief among them was my partner, the second-largest shareholder, who had been left jobless after losing his position at the telecommunications company. So I let it continue, so long as it did not burden me with further losses.

But later, I began to sense the perilous state of the company amidst turbulent markets and a lack of information. I pushed relentlessly to uncover the truth, but my partner—the one holding the reins—

was a master of delay and evasion. I even hired a private auditor to assess the company's condition and prepare a report laying bare the reality. Yet he couldn't complete his task because my partner withheld the crucial data. So I brought in another man, known for his unyielding resolve, hoping he would succeed where the first had failed. But he, too, hit a dead end.

Evidently, my partner had been grappling with financial strain due to other business ventures—despite being a real estate tycoon who had never faced money troubles before, even after acquiring additional company shares. But as the saying goes: "Nothing lasts forever." This was what drove him to flee the country without prior warning or notice, leaving me the very next day in a disaster with no beginning or end—an unbearably difficult situation. Suddenly, I found myself responsible for salvaging a company in pitiable condition. I vowed to rescue the company from its wretched condition, if only to mitigate the impending damage that would inevitably befall me.

I set about piecing things together and straightening out the company's affairs. With time—and the help of a new accountant—I managed to bring order to the company's operations to a considerable degree, settling numerous claims and debts. The business was on the verge of regaining its stability, just as life seemed to be smiling at me again. Then, abruptly, the telecommunications company shut down

Hadara. They merged its operations with their parent company, nullifying the agreement that had tied us to Hadara—our sole remaining source of revenue. It was late 2021. There was no choice left but to close the company. I had indeed already initiated the closure procedures at the time, yet the process demands considerable time and formalities that continue to this very day.

That new accountant proved to be a true ally in relieving me of this burdensome file. He worked diligently in the final stages to properly close the accounts in coordination with the external auditor. Yet alas, he suddenly passed away—may God have mercy on him—in the prime of his youth, dealing yet another blow to the company and to me personally. His untimely death further delayed the process of freeing myself from this ordeal, both psychologically and financially draining.

This series of tragedies, setbacks, and disappointments formed an unrelenting chain of anguish that grew increasingly suffocating—a grim harbinger of a new cycle of lean years looming on the horizon.

Now, it's true that the first of those betrayals, however brutal, was something I could endure. I was still at the helm of my work, and I paid the sum my partner had extorted from me—the very man I had shown kindness to time and again, even from my own pocket. The same went for the second blow: that veiled coercion which forced me to buy worthless shares out of fear of the consequences had I refused.

As for my third partner—the one who held the second-largest stake in the company—what he did was leap from the boat, leaving me to drown in a raging sea of crises, all of his own making. His betrayal marked the beginning of an endless cycle of anguish, one that nearly suffocated me to death. Had I not steadied myself, reminding myself that every problem has a solution—and that if no solution exists, then there is no real problem to begin with—I might have been lost. After all, any problem solvable with money is, by definition, surmountable.

I continued my work of stabilizing the company's affairs with quiet and patience. Yet when the telecom company terminated its contract with Hadara Corporation—cutting off our primary source of income—what was meant to be a productive venture for my post-retirement years collapsed. This came just after my own contract with the telecom company had ended. It became the greatest of disappointments, the most crushing of setbacks, a spiral of anguish.

Yet the ordeal did not end there. The accursed COVID-19 pandemic swept through our lives, followed by a devastating war whose consequences proved even more cruel than the plague itself. Now every door swings open to uncertainty—more setbacks, more heartbreaks—and this cycle of suffering will likely persist through seven lean years. God alone knows what awaits at its end, before the darkness lifts and this ring of anguish at last breaks apart.

Just yesterday morning, I was wandering around Gamal Abdul Nasser Park in the heart of Nablus, drowning in worry and turning over those possibilities in my mind. The images of negative thinking had nearly overwhelmed me, threatening to darken the vision of the years to come—so much so that I saw myself standing at the door of a mosque, lifting my hands in supplication, 'For the sake of God, O charitable ones…'

Yet my destiny led me—without any power or effort of my own—to a walking Quran upon the earth, a virtuous man from whose lips I heard kindness and light that dispelled the darkness. He planted within my soul a new hope, one that—God willing—would be enough to shatter the encircling waves of pain, no matter how fierce or unrelenting. As for me, I would turn to seeking forgiveness, that God might lift from me this anguish and tribulation, for the two can never coexist, as they say. And so I wait, until the heavens rain upon me their bounty and blessings.

The End

Epilogue

Khalil Moh'd Khalil Hamad

About the Author

Khalil Hamad was born in 1954 in Palestine. Two years after his birth, he lost his mother and did not know her features; she didn't leave a picture. At the age of seven, he was shaken again when he suddenly learned that the woman, he called mother was his aunt. At the age of thirteen, the occupation began, and he saw the first bird hovering in the sky of the village. It was a huge helicopter flying at a low altitude, spreading terror in the place. He completed his secondary education under the shadow of war and fear. He moved to the city of Bethlehem, where he studied English literature at the university. He traveled to Kuwait to work and then to the United States to complete his studies, where he obtained a master's degree in comparative literature. There, he completed his master's thesis, which included his theory on "interpreting creative energy and the relationship between the orphan and creativity." This topic has always occupied him and continues and was the motivation behind writing his first book, "Let's Destroy the Idols of the Twenty-First Century." He also published a book called "Orphans: Projects of Great People," in which he confirmed, based on his discovery that there is a relationship between the orphan and creativity at its highest levels, that every orphan is in fact a great project.... He concluded by proposing a national plan to care for the orphans.... the great people of the future.

Inner Child Press

Inner Child Press is a publishing company founded and operated by writers. Our personal publishing experiences provide us an intimate understanding of the sometimes-daunting challenges writers, new and seasoned may face in the business of publishing and marketing their creative "Written Work".

For more information:

Inner Child Press

www.innerchildpress.com

intouch@innerchildpress.com

building bridges of cultural understanding
www.innerchildpress.com

www.ingramcontent.com/pod-product-compliance
Lightning Source LLC
Chambersburg PA
CBHW070220030726
47505CB00006B/1738